THE PRAIRIETON RAID

Also by Lauran Paine

THE PRAIRIETON RAID

Lauran Paine

Walker and Company
New York

First published in the United States of America in 1994 by Walker
Publishing Company, Inc.

Published simultaneously in Canada by Thomas Allen & Son Canada,
Limited, Markham, Ontario

Library of Congress Cataloging-in-Publication Data
Paine, Lauran.
The Prairieton raid / Lauran Paine.
p.   cm.
ISBN 0-8027-4139-8
1. Outlaws—West (U.S.)—Fiction.   I. Title.
PS3566.A34P72   1994
813'.54—dc20   94-1232
CIP

Printed in the United States of America

2   4   6   8   10   9   7   5   3

Contents

THE PRAIRIETON RAID

CHAPTER ONE

The Arrival of Spring

THREE MEN SAT their horses on the timbered sidehill above the open country overlooking the town of Prairieton, in the center of Pawnee Valley.

From where they sat, the view was of an ocean of grassland surrounded by mountains so distant they almost appeared to be heat-hazed mirages.

Henry Malden, a thin-lipped man with carrot hair, a long nose, and steel-gray eyes, shifted in his saddle. Buff Brady had ridden out from Prairieton to meet his two partners. He gave them his scouting report. ". . . Three roads. One due south, the other two east and west."

Boice Candless removed his roping gloves to roll a smoke. He was a deliberate individual, unhurried, never very talkative, and gave the impression of shrewd thoughtfulness. Boice was a 'breed, with dark, curly hair and the build of a blacksmith. "We can come back to camp after we've seen things are about like Buff said."

Henry fished for his plug and worried off a corner before saying to his companions, "Better not ride in together."

Candless grunted, and squeezed his horse with both knees. He led the way down off the slope to where they could blend into the backdrop of gloomy forest. Boice and Henry left their partner and headed south toward town. Approaching from this direction, across the mountains south, was something people did not do unless they en-

1

joyed extreme hardship. More likely they chose the course to evade others, including possemen.

Their animals were tucked up but hardened through weeks of use. Up yonder there had been several lightning-made clearings with grass and water in them, providing sustenance to keep the horses going, but not enough to put an ounce of fat on them.

When Boice and Henry left the timber for open country they rode into warm sunshine. They surmised that either summer had arrived abruptly in Pawnee Valley or this particular day was unusually hot.

The two riders split up about three miles north of Prairieton—Boice heading east, Henry west. They planned to meet later at the livery barn, located at the southern end of town opposite the blacksmith's shop. According to Buff, the livery barn was across the pole corrals from the Prairieton jailhouse.

There was nothing particularly outstanding about Prairieton, except for the big red-brick bank opposite the saloon and the sycamore trees lining Main street.

The town may have had a long history, as did most that were situated at the hub of converging roads in open country, but there was no evidence now of Prairieton ever having been a hide depot or a well-watered place for freighters to rendezvous. Whatever log buildings had once been there were sided over with planed lumber. This was now the kind of town people settled in without any thought of moving on.

Prairieton was largely supported by the cattle trade and was surrounded by large ranches. For cattlemen, the biggest drawback was that when the railroad entered the country, it did not come this far. They had to drive cattle forty miles south and load rail cars from Edgerton's shipping corrals.

With no railroad, Prairieton lacked another vestige of

progress: It had no telegraph facility. That too was down at Edgerton.

But the town had survived well enough.

The livery barn was one of several businesses in town. The owner, Ed Duval, was sufficiently satisfied with his new dayman to treat him almost as an equal. The dayman worked hard, said little, and had an unusually sound knowledge of horseflesh. Buff Brady was the best hostler Ed had hired since he'd bought the livery seven years earlier.

As Ed had told Marshal Will Mosher, he hoped the dayman would never leave. Coming from Ed Duval, whose ordinarily disparaging attitude was well known, this was praise the marshal could not ignore. So he had decided he'd go down and meet the dayman.

Buff was just outside the harness room, cleaning bridles, when Mosher ambled in. Marshal Mosher had no difficulty in striking up a conversation. The marshal was experienced in drawing people out, and the new dayman seemed to be an open, amiable individual, so they talked for a half hour while the hostler worked and Will sat on a bench at the north wall of the runway outside the harness room.

Buff Brady said he hailed from New Mexico. The reason he had taken the hostler's job, he told the marshal, was because although he had tried most of the local cow outfits, it was a tad late in the season and they had their full complements of seasonal riders.

Buff was young, affable, and sinewy from years of working out of doors. He smiled ruefully as he said he thought the real reason he hadn't been hired was because ranchers preferred to hire local riders.

Mosher nodded and told the new dayman that next season he should start hunting work earlier. With stockmen unsure of what might come along later, they would probably hire him.

"If I'm still in the country," Buff said, agreeing with the

advice. "Where I come from, it stays warm year round most of the time. Up here in Colorado they tell me it gets cold early, snows hard, and don't let up until maybe April or May."

Mosher asked, "What part of New Mexico you from?"

The dayman, who had never been in New Mexico, answered easily. "Mostly, all over. Rode for a lot of outfits down there."

The marshal watched Buff drape a cleaned bridle over a coffee tin nailed to the wall and line up the next one. "Ed says you know horses," he said.

"Ought to. Been around them since I was a button. My pa traded, and sometimes I went along with him. But it's a hard way to serve the lord, Marshal. You should have seen some of the ringers folks sold him, swearin' up an' down they was good, trustworthy animals. I got so used to gettin' bucked off I'd land on my feet."

Mosher knew about that too. "A man gets so's he can tell a splint or sidebone, or tell when a horse is wind broke, but I been around them all my life, too, and I can't tell what's inside their heads."

Buff Brady worked, sweated, and let the conversation lapse. Eventually the marshal shoved up to his feet as he said, "Well, Ed's got his shortcomings, but taken all in all, if you don't take nothin' off him, you'll have a job as long as you want it."

On his way out, Marshal Mosher nodded to a stranger who had just appeared out front, a red-haired man with a long nose. Henry Malden stood with the reins in his hand, watching the lawman stride toward the jailhouse office. When Malden went inside the livery barn, Buff Brady kept right on cleaning bridles. As the steel-eyed man led his horse down the cool runway, Buff looked up and nodded.

Henry stopped and stood hipshot, watching for a moment, then went to work skiving off a sliver of chewing tobacco with a razor-sharp clasp knife.

Buff asked, "Where's Boice?"

He got no reply until the other man had cheeked his cud and expectorated. "We split up out yonder. He'll be along directly." For a moment the tobacco chewer watched Buff at work, then said dryly, "Is this the best you could do?"

Buff turned with a rueful smile. "I don't know. It was the first place I asked. You want to put up your horse?"

Malden shrugged, stepped back, and began tugging his latigo loose. He carried the saddle into the harness room and returned to halter the horse and remove its bridle. "Any particular stall?"

"No." Buff turned to watch Henry stall the animal, fork some feed to it, and stroll back to where Buff was finishing the last bridle.

Malden chewed, watched, then tipped his hat back, shifted his shell belt, and said, "I'll be at the cafe." He walked back out into the sunlight.

Buff took a coffee can of rolled barley to Henry's horse and went out back to roll and light a smoke. He scanned the countryside with no particular anxiety. He was confident Boice would be along.

While he was out there, he saw a very pretty woman walk from a residence to the rear yard and begin hanging laundry on a taut old lariat. She did not see him.

When he finished his smoke and went back inside, Ed Duval was standing in the harness-room doorway. "You clean them bridles?" he asked.

Buff nodded. "They needed it."

Ed went over to the bench and sat down about where the town marshal had sat. He eyed the dayman in front of him for a moment before saying, "Go up to the saloon if you like. It's gettin' along toward supper time."

Buff looked at the fat, pale-eyed man. "Never was much of a drinkin' man, Mister Duval."

The liveryman sighed. Every hostler he'd ever hired had been a drinking man. For that matter so was the liveryman.

He shrugged and said, "No need to hang around anymore today. See you in the morning."

After his dayman had departed, Ed continued to sit and cogitate. This feller was too good to be true. There had to be a hole in him somewhere.

Ed went into the harness room, examined the bridles, then sat down on a rickety old swivel chair that had been stoutly reinforced to hold his weight. He leaned with a grunt to get a bottle of whiskey from a lower drawer, took two swallows, and put the bottle back.

Someone had just ridden up, so Ed went out front. He exchanged nods with the burly rangeman and reached for the man's reins as he said, "Grained an' hayed an' stalled?"

"Not stalled," Boice Candless replied. "Hayed and grained and corralled."

"Gets stocked-up, does he?"

Boice replied shortly, "I just don't like to stall a horse unless it's real bad weather."

"All right. You figure on leavin' in the morning?"

Boice looked darkly at the fat man, turned, and walked out of the runway. Ed Duval shrugged; every now and then someone would come along who didn't like being asked questions. That was all right with Ed. He didn't like questions either. But it made it easier knowing how long someone wanted to leave his animal.

After he had taken care of the stranger's horse, he went back out front and saw Jeremy Blanding about to enter the cafe. They exchanged a wave, not a very warm one on either side.

Duval leaned on the side of the runway's wide doorless opening. He did not like Jeremy Blanding, not just because he always wore britches and coats that matched, along with a tie around his neck, to make a point about being the local banker, but also because Blanding neither drank nor smoked nor swore. The liveryman considered that unnatural, maybe excluding the preachers who came to town now and then to bellow about hellfire and brimstone and to pass the hat.

It had been the liveryman's intention to head for the cafe, but after seeing Blanding go in over there he decided to wait.

He went back down to the harness room, eyed the stranger's outfit, then went out back to look at his horse.

It had a shoulder brand Ed had never seen before, but then, that was not unusual. The horse was a sound, tough, powerful animal, with little eyes and a slightly roman nose. He gave the impression he could come across those damned northern mountains and still have enough "bottom" left to rope calves through whatever was left of the day.

Ed returned to the harness room, which was also his office. He sat down and fingered through his fly-specked ledger, a chore he hated. He traded horses, cared for them, and upon occasion used one of his wagons to haul local freight. Hunching over ledger books was anathema to him.

He decided he was making a profit—not from the book, but from intuition—and headed for the cafe.

The banker had eaten and departed. Otherwise the counter was about half full. It was a tad early; the sun was still above the westerly rims. The cafe would fill up when local businesses closed down for the night.

Ed ordered his usual supper: steak, fried spuds, and black coffee. He would top it off later with a big slice of apple pie.

The cafeman eyed him askance. Unless Ed did more work and cut down on his eats, he was going to get so damned fat that if he fell down he'd rock himself to sleep trying to get up.

CHAPTER TWO
Settling In

PRAIRIETON'S BLACKSMITH WAS a wiry evil-dispositioned man named Tony Halderman. He never lighted cigars, he chewed them. His temper was notorious over the countryside, but he was a good man with horseshoes, wagon tires, sprung axles, or just about anything that had to do with his trade.

Over the years he'd had no less than twenty helpers. They invariably quit because of Halderman's temper. As Ed Duval had once said to Kent Overman, who operated Prairieton's only saloon, Halderman was so mean that hell wouldn't have him.

Kent was a beefy, easygoing, balding man who avoided taking sides, because it was bad for business. He had nodded toward the liveryman, neither agreeing nor disagreeing.

His saloon was called the Palace; two-thirds of the cow towns west of the Missouri had a "Palace" saloon. Kent had a good business. He made his own beer, which most of the time was very good. When a batch turned out bad, his patrons let him know. He was also the local clearinghouse for information about everything, from who needed riders in the surrounding countryside to who in town was expecting, or drinking too much.

When a red-haired stranger asked where he might find some work, Overman sent him down to the smithy. Halderman, warping a tire around a wheel and chewing a cigar as he worked, did not see the man leaning in the shop doorway until he stepped back from fitting shims to wipe his hands on a dirty canvas apron. They exchanged a long look before Henry Malden nodded and said he'd heard the blacksmith needed a hired hand.

Halderman looked Henry up and down, removed his stogie to expectorate, then pointed to the wheel on its jig, and said, "Finish it. Maybe we'll talk."

Henry removed his shell belt and hat, draped them from a peg, rolled up his sleeves, and went to work. Halderman sat on an old horseshoe keg, watching. Malden released the jig, grounded the wheel, and trundled it to the big vat of dirty water. When he hoisted it and let it down into the water, Halderman made up his mind. The smithy walked over to where Henry was drying his hands and said, "You're hired. How much wages you been getting?"

Henry smiled into the other man's closed, bitter face as he said, "Six dollars a week."

Halderman would have paid ten. "Where you from?"

Henry's smile lingered. "Here an' there. Mostly there. Been a rangeman the last couple of years."

"When you want to start work?"

Henry looked at the soaking wheel. "Right now. Tomorrow, if that'd suit you better."

"It wouldn't suit me better. Finish that wheel. You any good shoeing?"

"I've done my share, an' maybe someone else's share too."

Halderman removed his apron, handed it to the hired man, and said, "Couple of thousand-pound harness horses in the corral out back. They belong to the stage company an' they want them by this evening. I got some chores to do. See you later."

Henry watched the blacksmith leave the shop and turn northward. The Palace was up there. He shrugged, went out back to look at the horses, then returned to the dingy, sooted interior and went to work on the wheel.

Later, when he was trimming the feet of one of the big horses, Ed Duval came over, leading a nice blood-bay gelding. He asked where Halderman was.

Henry looked up from his hunched position. "Said he had some chores to do. You want that horse shod? Put him in one of the corrals out back."

Ed dutifully took the horse on through to the corrals. That stranger inside the shop was about as curt as Halderman. It would be interesting to see how long this one lasted.

Halderman leaned on the bar, nursing a jolt glass of popskull as he explained to Overman how he had just hired the stranger the barkeep had sent down to his shop.

Kent, who knew the blacksmith as well as anyone, was cautious. "He didn't seem all that young to me, Tony. Most of the fellers who've worked for you—"

"What in the hell has age to do with it?" Halderman exclaimed. "You know how long I been in the smithy business?"

"No."

"Thirty years, man an' boy."

"What I meant was—"

"I know what you meant, gawddamit. You meant older fellers should be settin' in the sun, not workin' at a trade that's harder than a feller like you would know about."

Kent waited until Halderman had downed his shot, then he said placatingly, "All I meant was that that feller looked to be about my age."

Halderman snorted. "Let me tell you something, Kent—a blacksmith's got to have some age on him. I never seen one yet who could swell a wheel his first day on the job like that feller can. By the way, I forgot to ask his name. You know it?"

"Nope. Didn't ask. He bought a drink, we talked for a few minutes, an' he left."

Halderman held up his little glass for a refill. As Kent was reaching to the back bar for the bottle, the blacksmith said, "This one's goin' to stay, if I got to pay him double."

Kent did not reply, but he knew they never stayed; if they didn't quit, Halderman fired them. Two weeks, he told himself. A month at the longest.

The following week Kent Overman was dunking some glasses in the tub of greasy water behind the bar when Marshal Mosher walked in. They exchanged a nod and the big, thick lawman settled against the bar and called for a beer. After Overman brought it, the marshal said, "Remember that stringbean of a coachman Andy fired for bein' drunk on the run from Edgerton last month?"

Kent remembered, because the stage driver had left town owing a respectable bar bill. "Asa Stringfellow? Yeah, I remember him. Is he back?"

"Not that I know of. Andy just hired another driver to replace him. A 'breed-lookin' big feller named Boice Candless."

Kent shook his head to indicate he had never heard of anyone named Boice Candless. He asked if the corralyard boss had sent the new driver out yet, and Mosher nodded.

"Sent him out on a run a few days ago. Andy said the only way you could separate the wheat from the chaff was to send one out. By the time they got back, he'd know whether he'd made a mistake or not."

Kent made a swipe of the bartop with a sour-smelling rag. "For bein' as young as he is, Andy's smart enough."

The lawman sipped his beer before speaking again. "Yeah. Jeremy Blanding's a pretty good judge of men. He's the one who got Andy the job."

Kent allowed himself a disparaging remark, something he rarely did. "Blanding's got money invested in the stage company and he's always trying to run everybody else's business."

Will Mosher smiled, "What in this town hasn't he got money invested in?"

"This here saloon," Kent replied with spirit. "If Jeremy Blanding was all that stood between me an' leavin' town on foot with a bundle on my back, I'd leave town."

The marshal finished his beer and returned to the roadway. Across the road in front of the bank, Blanding and a local cowman named Chester Grant were talking. The banker was shaking his head as he spoke. Marshal Mosher knew Chester Grant; he had a large cow outfit, but just about everything that could go wrong for a man had gone wrong for Chester Grant for about a year. Rustlers had made off with over two hundred of his best cows, feed had come up short for what was left, and last summer a prairie fire had wiped out most of his range.

It required no particular intuition to surmise that Chester wanted a loan and Jeremy Blanding was refusing it.

The marshal went down to the jailhouse, sifted through some mail the clerk had brought over from the general store, and filed a half dozen Wanted dodgers in a box in his storeroom without even looking at them. They came in handy during winter for firing up kindling in the office stove.

He was thinking about going over to the cafe, when an unwashed, stalwart, nearly toothless man walked in. Forrest Kindig was a local pot hunter; he killed game in the northward mountains, dressed it out, and brought it in on a packhorse to peddle around town. The cafe owner was his best customer.

All anyone knew about Kindig was that he lived somewhere in the mountains. Rumor had it that he was one of the last vestiges of the old-time buffalo hunters. He dressed in greasy home-tanned buckskin and moccasins.

Will Mosher pointed to a chair, which the older man

took. Obeying manners established a generation earlier, Kindig led up to the purpose of his visit by mentioning the weather, the condition of the grazing country, even a little about politics, which, in his case—since he could neither read nor had access to any vocal opinions—was usually ten years behind the times.

Eventually he said, "Takes a real good horse to come through them northern mountains, Marshal. Specially this time of year, when there's still snow up there. Takes real good men too, I'd say, maybe with some reason to do that.

"From the sign, three fellers come over and down this side about a week or ten days ago." Kindig paused to allow the innuendo to sink in, then continued, "They made a camp a mile or such a matter above the open country. They ain't been around for a spell. They left their bedrolls, some pans, an' whatnot up there like they'd be comin' back, only they ain't. I been keepin' watch on their camp for most of a week."

The lawman was not very impressed. "Hunters, maybe, Forrest. Pot hunters. Scoutin' around for a few days. They'll come back. A man don't go off an' leave his bedroll."

"How about rustlers, Marshal? That camp's just far enough back to be invisible from down below, an' they was up there several days. Rustlers would act like that. Keep out of sight while they're pokin' around, studyin' out where to round up and make off with cattle. This time of year with grass comin' on, stockmen don't have no reason to be watchin' their critters very close."

Marshal Mosher considered the suggestion, decided it would do no harm to find the camp, and asked the pot hunter how to locate it. Getting directions from someone who knew every yard of the mountains and described the location of the camp in mountaineer terms was not very helpful to him, so Mosher asked how long Kindig would be in town. The hunter had sold all his meat and was on his way back as soon as he walked out of the jailhouse office. That posed a problem. If Mosher left town with the hunter, it would be dark before they reached the foothills, and while Kindig could probably locate the camp in darkness, the prospect of riding all night, cold and probably on a wild-goose chase, had no particular appeal. Mosher said, "Give me the general location an' I'll ride up in a day or two."

The "general location" was as ambiguous as Will Mosher had expected, but at least he knew the lower country well enough from hunting up there every autumn to know at least some of the area Kindig described.

Mosher's last words to him were to be very careful about nosing around the camp. If the men who had established it were, as Kindig had implied, rustlers or some other variety of unsavory individuals, Kindig could get himself shot.

After the pot hunter departed, Marshal Mosher went over in his mind about where he thought that camp had to be. But he was not convinced it had been established by the kind of men the pot hunter had said. Even if they actually had crossed the mountains, that did not prove they were up to no good.

He was not enthusiastic about going up there, but he would do it to satisfy his own curiosity, only not for a while. There was enough to look after in town; nothing threatening or even suspicious, but he was a *town* marshal, not a far-ranging federal officer or a county sheriff.

CHAPTER THREE
Something Unexpected

HENRY MALDEN WAS finishing work on the liveryman's blood bay when Duval's dayman strolled over in the late afternoon to get the horse.

Malden nodded impassively and continued the final rasping as he said, "Six dollars a week an' he's a cranky old bastard."

Buff Brady sat on the little horseshoe keg and smiled. He looked around, squinted in the direction of the rear yard with its scrap heap and corrals, and asked where the blacksmith was.

Malden straightened up slowly; blacksmithing was hell on a man's back. "Up at the saloon, I'd guess. From what I've heard, the barman's about his only friend in town. Why? You supposed to see him?"

"No. I wondered if it's safe in here."

Malden turned, untied his leather apron, and nodded. "It's safe. Where's Boice?"

"Hired on with the stage company. Out on a run, most likely won't be back until tomorrow."

Henry scowled. "He should have got hired somewhere we could count on him."

Buff shrugged. "He can beg off or get sick or something. We're supposed to meet up at the camp. I'll try and meet him when he gets back. Maybe we could meet up yonder day after tomorrow."

Henry's scowl faded, but he was still unhappy. "*If* he can

get off for a day. Hard to do when you're just startin' on a new job."

Buff nodded slightly. "I can get off day after tomorrow. How about you?"

Henry was rolling the shoeing apron when he replied. "Halderman won't like it, but I'll figure out something."

Henry handed the shank of the blood bay to Brady and went to rinse his hands and arms in the tub used for quenching and soaking. As he turned to wipe off with a large blue bandana, he asked, "You been inside yet?"

"No. You?"

"Not yet, but I'll make it first chance I get. We only been here a week. We got time."

Buff eyed the blood bay. A tractable, handsome animal, a tad light for the average man, more suitable for a woman. Buff said offhandedly, "I got our animals in a big corral. Feedin' 'em good and grainin' 'em."

The older man perched on an anvil. "Pretty town," he said. "When I settle down, I'd like to be in a place like this."

Buff turned from the horse. "Someday," he said, and led the horse out into the late-day sunshine.

Ed Duval saw him crossing the road and caught up with him as he was cuffing the blood bay before turning him out. Ed complimented himself again for hiring Brady. The damned horse would roll in corral dust as soon as he was turned out, but for a fact a good cuffing got rid of scurf, the prime cause of itching backs.

Ed trailed Buff out back, waited while the blood bay was turned in and the gate was closed, then settled comfortably against the peeled log stringers and smiled. He was in an expansive mood. "You don't have to go lookin' for work," he said. "There's time now'n then for a man to set down for a spell."

Buff smiled back. "As a matter of fact, Mister Duval, if you got no objections, I'd like to take some time off day after tomorrow."

Ed said, "Sure. Fine." Then it occurred to him his new dayman, being a rider by trade, might have in mind looking for work among the ranches again. He said, "Gettin' late in the season on the ranches."

Buff nodded as though he had not caught the implication. "I like the country. Thought I'd ride out an' around, look over the territory. Seems like it might be good country to settle down in."

Ed's relief was almost perceptible. "It is," he exclaimed. "Nice town, pretty setting, good folks, an' the countryside's about as nice as a man can find. I been here a number of years an' never had no hankering to move on."

They returned to the runway, where a thick-necked man with a mass of wavy gray hair worn long was standing near the harness room, looking annoyed. Buff recognized him at once and nodded, but Ed Duval did better. He broke into an unctuous smile as he addressed the elegantly-suited individual.

"Mister Blanding, you want your buggy? I been meanin' to come up to the bank an' tell you I think the mare needs new shoes. Her feet are getting pretty long."

The large, unpleasant-looking man stared at the liveryman. "All right. Get her shod. And Ed, have Tony come up to the bank for his money."

"Yes indeed, Mister Blanding. First thing in the morning. Oh, by the way, this here is my new dayman, Buff Brady."

Buff waited for a hand, which was not extended. The banker gazed at Buff, barely inclined his head, then addressed the liveryman again. "I need the buggy, Ed."

"Yes, sir. Buff, fetch in that seal-brown mare across the alley in the private corral. I'll pull the rig inside." As Buff turned to obey, Ed said, "Have a seat on that bench behind you, Mister Blanding. This won't take long."

Buff was haltering the docile big mare, who looked to be one of those stud-necked Oregon horses out of remount stock, when Ed Duval went toward the runway from the buggy shed, pulling a nice top buggy with yellow wheels.

Ed put a new harness on the big mare. Buff held the shafts up as she was backed between them. Blanding sat on the bench, watching indifferently. "Real nice weather we're having," Ed said. "No rain for some weeks. Us folks in town like that, but the cowmen sure won't."

Blanding did not appear to be listening. He took some papers from an inside coat pocket, studied them briefly, and put them back into the pocket.

Ed tried again. "Completin' that trans-continental railroad is something to think about, ain't it? A man can get on the steam cars in New York and ride all the way to California. Hard to believe, eh?"

Blanding eyed the fat liveryman dispassionately and addressed Buff Brady. "Where you from?"

"New Mexico, but this is sure pretty country. A man could do worse than to settle here," Buff replied amiably.

Blanding removed a large golden watch, snapped the case open, consulted the spidery black hands, and snapped the case closed. As he pocketed the watch, he said, "Don't seem to me our country needs any more livery-barn hostlers."

He accepted the lines from a red-faced Ed Duval, led the rig out front before climbing in, and turned northward up through town.

Ed wiped sweat off, went up as far as the front barn opening, and watched the yellow wheels spin dust to life. Behind him Buff said, "Real likable feller, Mister Duval."

Ed turned, showing an entirely different expression. "Don't call me Mister Duval. Just Ed."

"All right."

"Someday," stated the fat man, "someday that measly bastard'll get his comeuppance, and I hope I'm around to see it."

Buff's reply was softly said. "You most likely will be. Does anyone like him?"

"I guess his wife does, poor little critter. More'n likely she's scairt of the son of a bitch. Plenty of folks are, especially them as owe the bank money, like me. I'll give you a word of advice, Buff. If you can possibly avoid it, don't ever borrow money from his bank. The minute you do, he looks down on you like you was dirt, even when you make payments on time. Even when you pay off the loan."

Brady turned back down the runway. It was time to start forking feed. He worked for sometime before pausing to lean on his pitchfork.

That evening he visited the Palace. Henry Malden was already there, and to Buff's surprise, as well as the surprise of everyone else, the blacksmith's new hired man was drinking with his employer, something no one had seen Tony Halderman ever do before. He was by habit, and perhaps preference, a solitary after-hours drinker.

Buff's eyes met Henry's.

The saloon was almost full. All it lacked were the stockmen from beyond town, but this was not Saturday night.

Kent Overman knew the liveryman's hired hand by sight, and as he came down the bar, he smiled. He had reason to; everything he'd heard so far about Buff Brady had been good. He nodded after receiving Buff's order and went after a bottle and small glass. It was a busy night; he could not linger.

Buff slowly filled the glass, catching a brief glimpse of himself in the back-bar mirror as he threw back his head and downed the liquor.

Two older men on his right side were talking. One wore black cotton sleeve-protectors from wrist to elbow, common practice with men who worked at desks or clerked in stores. He was older, lined and watery-eyed. He was wondering to his shorter and nearly bald companion why Marshal Mosher had left town about sunrise, when the old man was unlocking the doors of the emporium. The marshal had been bundled in a heavy coat and had a carbine slung under his *rosadero* as he headed north out of town.

The balding man took time out to down a straight jolt of raw whiskey before replying. His voice rasped as he said, "Where in hell does Kent get this stuff? It smells like arsenic an' tastes like coal oil. Will Mosher? I heard that greasy old toothless pot hunter who peddles meat around town tellin' folks he found a hidden camp up in the foothills with no one around, but with camp gear still on the ground. The old hunter said it could be outlaws or somethin' because he backtracked an' found that them fellers had crossed the damned mountains. I seen the old cuss go into the jailhouse, so my guess is that he got Will to ride up there an' look around."

The tall, older man turned his little jolt glass in a sticky circle. "You can't believe what them old gaffers say. They been livin' up in them canyons, lookin' at nothin' but rocks an' trees so long they get about half loco in the head."

Kent came down the bar. Buff paid up and returned to the roadway. The town was mostly dark. Down at Duval's barn the pair of carriage lamps had been lighted, one on each side of the wide, doorless front opening.

Across the road at the bank building, the steel shutters had been closed and a brass lock as large as a man's fist hung from the roadside door.

Buff went up to the rooming house. The proprietor was sitting out front on the porch, smoking a pipe. He nodded to Buff as he said, "Evenin'."

Buff nodded and headed to his room down a poorly lighted corridor. Inside, he lighted a hanging lamp. Then he tossed his hat aside, draped his shell belt and holstered Colt from a wall peg, and sat down to build a smoke.

An hour later, when the ramshackle old structure was silent, Buff went down to Malden's room and knocked on the door.

Within moments the door swung open and Malden stood there with one hand behind his back, puffy-faced but alert.

Buff pushed past and waited until Malden had closed the door and returned his six-gun to its holster before he began relating what he had heard at the saloon.

Henry went to the edge of his bed and sat down, scratching his head. He scowled at Buff. "I told you'n Boice when we was still a mile or so uphill that I smelled smoke."

Buff did not respond.

"One thing's a damned cinch: we can't go back to that camp."

Buff had already thought about that. What worried him now was that if they had left something behind that the marshal could use to identify any of them, they would be in trouble, not just for what they planned for Prairieton, but for things they'd already done.

Henry shook his head. "All he'll find is three bedrolls and some cookin' pans. That don't worry me, Buff. What does, is what might have happened if we'd went up there and met him. Things are gettin' a little close to the chest. We got to get hold of Boice."

"Can't do that until he returns tomorrow," Buff stated. "Keep watch from the smithy for a returning coach an' I'll do the same from the barn. So much for us not bein' seen together."

"We can manage that. Only one of us'll go talk to him, an' we got to do it like it's a casual meeting."

Buff went to the door and stood there, looking back. He said nothing. Malden arose from the edge of the bed and shook his head. "Well, it's not the first time we've had to figure fast. Most likely it won't be the last. Thank gawd you was at the saloon tonight."

"Henry?"

"What."

"That town marshal don't seem real lively to me. I talked

to him awhile, down at the barn. I got the feelin' that he'd rather set here in town than do a lot of horse-backing."

"I've seen 'em like that before—half asleep until someone sticks a burr under their saddle blanket. Then they come to life."

"He won't find nothin' up yonder, then he'll come back and get busy in town again. But it won't do no harm to watch the son of a bitch, will it?"

Malden nodded, and after Buff slipped back out into the dark corridor, he returned to bed.

Fortunately his occupation was one that left a tired body at night. He went back to sleep and did not awaken until the sun was coming. It was too late for him to eat breakfast, so he hurriedly visited the washhouse out back and strode past the cafe directly to the smithy where what he had thought might not happen, had happened: Tony Halderman was already at work and his first cigar of the day was cocked at a menacing angle.

The moment Henry walked in, Halderman glared and pointed to a badly sprung axle that belonged to the stage company. Then he went back to work without saying a word.

Malden fired the forge, got fresh quenching water, and ratted the axle clean over an anvil. He did not look at his employer, and Halderman did not look at him.

Straightening the axle was not difficult; it was the tempering after straightening that required skill and knowledge. He went about the tempering unaware that Halderman was watching everything he did from the corner of his eye.

When the axle was finished, all but running down the threads, Henry leaned it aside to cool, then turned and said, "Slept too hard last night."

Halderman was shaping a calked shoe and held his hammer aloft as he replied. "That's once. You eat?"

"No. I'll last until dinnertime."

"Go get breakfast, I don't want no man to go puny on me. We got horses to shoe when you get back."

Henry hesitated a moment, but Halderman would not look around, so he grunted as he passed the older man and went up to get fed.

CHAPTER FOUR
A Midnight Meeting

WHEN BOICE CANDLESS got back from his run, he beat dust off as he crossed to the Palace saloon. Before pushing inside, he stood a moment looking southward.

Buff saw him and, because Ed Duval was snoring in the office, he hurried up the back alley until he was opposite the saloon. Then he briskly crossed the road, entered the nearly empty saloon, and settled against the bar beside Boice. Kent brought him a tepid beer, the only kind he served, and went back to washing glasses up near the north end of the bar.

Neither Buff nor Boice looked at each other, but their eyes met in the bar mirror as Buff said, "We can't go back to the camp. Tell you about it later. I got room number eleven at the hotel. I'll leave the back window open. Henry an' I'll be up there about midnight."

Candless grunted and raised his glass to drain it as Buff left the saloon to hasten back to the lower end of town.

When Buff returned, Ed was still snoring. Buff got busy raking the private corral across the alley; the banker's big, docile mare watched with calm interest.

Later, when Ed came out back, drawn by the sound of raking, he leaned on the stringer and said, "Partner, you work too hard." It was the first time he'd ever said that to a hired man.

Buff paused to sleeve sweat off his face and smiled. "My

paw raised us boys to do things. He used to say doin' just about anythin' is better'n doin' nothing."

Duval had to hitch at his sagging britches. His paunch was getting to be quite a problem. "I got to go over to the emporium an' get a set of braces. Damned pants keep fallin' down. Be back directly."

Buff leaned on the rake, watching his boss go up the runway toward Main Street, and smiled. Across the road Malden came to the front opening of the smithy. He was wearing a smoke-tanned mulehide shoeing apron. When Henry saw him, Buff nodded, then they both went back to work.

An hour later Marshal Mosher turned in at the barn, dismounted stiffly, handed Buff his reins, and stretched mightily. He hadn't found any damned camp with bedrolls in it. He had quartered like a coon dog for almost two hours, until it was too dark, then he had rolled into the single army blanket behind his cantle and spent a miserable night before returning to town. He had a hint of salt-and-pepper beard stubble and was not in a very good mood. He and the dayman exchanged a minimum of words before Buff watched him head toward the jailhouse, his booted saddlegun over his shoulder like a chopping axe.

Across the way Henry Malden and his employer had a full quota of thousand-pound harness horses to shoe for the stage company. Mostly they worked in silence, but when Henry had finished his second animal and was leading the third one in to be cross-tied for shoeing, he studied the animal's feet, finished the tying, and leaned over. He looked, leaned lower, and ran a roughened hand over the near-side front hoof.

The animal was quiet, not apprehensive like many horses were when they had been cross-tied. Henry lifted the hoof, cleaned it with the pick from his rear pocket, examined it closely. Before pulling the worn shoes, he used a rasp to cut directly across and a tad above a barely noticeable crack.

Halderman had finished with his animal; he straightened up slowly, spat, and considered the splayed end of his stogie before pitching it into the forge. He watched Henry for a moment, then said, "What the hell are you doing?"

Henry replied without looking up from his rasping. "Filing over a quarter crack. What does it look like I'm doing?"

Halderman reddened, his nostrils flared. He moved over and looked, plugged a fresh stogie between his teeth, and without another word, went out back to bring in the next horse. He watched Henry dig into the soft part of the hoof with his knife, saw him palm several tiny bits of granite, and got to work on his own animal.

It required considerable time for Henry to shoe the animal with the quarter crack. He was still working on it when Halderman took his freshly shod animal out back to the corral and led in the next one. As he was tying this horse he scowled without looking around as he said, "We don't make no money babyin' 'em, Henry."

For a time Henry went right on working. When he was finally finished and was rinsing his hands and arms, he turned to watch Halderman briefly, then walked over and tapped him on his bent-over back. When Halderman looked up, Henry said, "You like horses, Mister Halderman?"

Very slowly the older man put the hoof down and straightened up. "What I like or don't like isn't none of your business. I hired you to—"

Without haste Malden reached, got a fistful of shirt, swung the blacksmith around, then released him. His voice was flat when he spoke. "Let a quarter crack like that go an' it'll get up into the coronet and maybe lame a good horse for life. I happen to like horses."

Halderman sputtered around his cigar. "We shoe horses here, we ain't vetinaries. You goin' to get back to work or ain't you?"

Henry was dead calm and expressionless as he regarded the other man. "Yeah, I'm goin' to get back to work. But first I'm goin' to tell you, old son of a bitch, you rag me one more time for doin' a good job where it's needed, an' I'll shove your head in that quenchin' tub until you drown."

Henry turned and went out back for his next horse, leaving Halderman red and fiery-eyed. When Henry walked back with a horse, they exchanged a look and Henry held up a warning finger, tied his horse, and went to work as though Halderman did not exist.

They did not exchange another word until just before quitting time. Henry had washed up and rolled down his sleeves, and Halderman was standing near his littered cubbyhole of an office. Henry walked up, looked him in the eye, and said, "You want to pay me off, do it now." He held out his palm.

Halderman got splotchy-faced again; his glare was fierce. He tongued the cigar from one side of his mouth to the other before saying, "I'll let you know when I'm goin' to pay you off. An' gawddammit, get down here earlier after this."

He left Henry standing there, ducked into the little office, and remained there until Henry was walking up in the direction of the rooming house. Then he came out of the office, craned up the north plankwalk, and swore fiercely with no one to hear him.

Henry did not go to his room; he went to the saloon. There was a scattering of men, mostly townsmen, along the bar when Henry bellied up and nodded for a bottle and glass. When Kent brought them they exchanged a look, and because Henry was still roiled, his gaze was smokily hostile. Kent went back up the bar and a large man eased in beside the blacksmith's helper and spoke quietly to him. "I was over in the livery barn," he said. "Me'n Ed heard you'n Tony all the way across the road."

Henry downed his drink without even looking around. The large man leaned down on the bar. "Folks know about his disposition."

Henry looked at the beefy man. It was the town marshal. His face was shiny, as though he'd just come from the tonsorial parlor. He smelled like it too; the Prairieton barber was liberal with his French toilet water when he finished a shearing. Henry wagged his head in a resigned manner.

"He's not hard to work for, if a man knows his business. But he's got a bad habit of raggin' folks. One of these days someone is goin' to yank the slack out of him."

Marshal Mosher was sympathetic, so he offered a warning. "Couple years ago a feller tried it. Tony's sort of stringy built, but he's faster'n a strikin' snake. He brained the feller with a wagon spoke."

Henry was beginning to feel mellow from his drink, so he grinned at the large man. "Thanks. I'll watch for wagon spokes."

He left the saloon, went down to the cafe to eat, then went up to his room to shed his shirt and hat. He went back to the washhouse, took a bath, and by the time he was dressing in the room, he was totally over his resentment. But intuition told him they would probably clash again, and Henry did not want to lose the job. Not yet, anyway.

With the sun teetering on distant spiky timbered rims, he strolled down the same side of Main Street as the bank and without breaking his stride, studied the steel shutters and the big brass padlock on the roadway door.

He went down almost as far as the jailhouse, crossed down through a dogtrot to the alley, and went to study the rear of the brick bank building. The rear door was bolted from the inside and there were no windows. Whoever had built the brick structure must have had a bank in mind:

there was only one way inside, and that was around in front. During daylight hours. Exactly at closing time.

A door could be blown open, but only once in his life had Henry been involved in anything like that, and the result had scarred his memory.

Before the echoes died and the smoke cleared, he and two companions had scooped up all the money they could find and fled. One was shot off his horse midway through town. The other one had been hit in the side, had managed to hang on for several miles, then Henry had led his horse into some rocks and helped the wounded man lie flat.

He was caught by ten possemen sitting with his dying friend. They got their money back, buried two outlaws in the local cemetary, and Henry had spent four years in the penitentiary.

A wizened old man at the penitentiary, who was to die there serving a life sentence for murder, had told Henry that if a man didn't learn from experience he was beyond hope.

He thought about going over to the saloon. There was plenty of time. Instead he returned to the hotel and knuckled Buff Brady's door. Buff told him about the meeting in his room at midnight, and Henry went along to his own room to cock back the only chair, cross his booted feet on the windowsill, meticulously slice a cud off his plug, cheek it, and think.

The big town marshal had not impressed him one way or the other. His mind wandered from one thing to another. He suspected the reason Halderman had not fired him was because he was as good a forge man as Halderman was, and was even better at shoeing horses, which he should have been; that had been the trade he had followed after prison—for five years, until he had met Buff and Boice. He was, in fact, as good a horseshoer as ever came down the pike. He had got that way because he liked horses, sympathized with them, and had never liked the cowboy-type of shoeing that was common, and which, in his opinion, probably lamed more good horses than just about anything else.

After dark he went out to sit on the veranda, where the night gloom was accentuated by a sagging overhang. At one corner of the old structure some noble soul had planted a wisteria bush years earlier. Its fragrance was almost overpowering.

He saw the marshal and a wispy, thin-haired man with an elegant gold watch chain across his vest conversing out front of the general store. He recognized the storekeeper, but the third man who joined them was unfamiliar to him.

Buff Brady came up and did not even look at Henry before entering the rooming house. Henry sat a while longer, until his cud had no molasses left in it, then jettisoned it in the direction of the wisteria bush, arose, and went back to his room.

He did not own a watch; instinct told him he had time for a nap, so he stretched out fully attired, tipped his hat over his face, and slept.

Buff went out back to clean up. He too had eaten earlier. When he returned to his room he locked the door and opened the rear window. The town noise lessened as time passed.

When Henry awakened, it was darker than the inside of a boot. He pushed the hat aside, perched on the edge of the bed for a moment, then went over to the window. Prairieton was mostly dark. The saloon had been locked up for the night and just about the only lights still burning were down in front of the liverybarn.

He left his shell belt and hat in the room, went over to Buff's door, and tapped gently. Somewhere farther along the corridor some drunk was singing between fits of coughing followed by lusty noises as he cleared his pipes.

Buff opened the door, stepped aside, closed it after Henry, and relocked it. Boice had not yet arrived.

Buff dug a bottle from under his pillow, but Henry declined and instead cheeked another cud of Kentucky twist. It was chilly with the window open, but neither man seemed to notice.

Boice arrived out of the darkness and had trouble getting his bulk through the window.

He had brought a bottle, too, but made no attempt to open it. Boice surprised them both by saying he had been inside the bank that afternoon. Andy Collins had asked him to take a money pouch down there to be counted out and deposited.

Buff was impressed. "One run an' he lets you handle money."

Boice placed a bland look on Brady. "We get along real well. I brought his hitch and coach back without a scratch and walked the horses the last two miles so's they'd be cooled out. I learnt some time back, drivin' stage up north, that what pleases corralyard bosses is not to have to cool out horses when they come in off a run."

Henry had a question. "When do you go out again?"

"First thing in the morning. Why? You ready?"

"No, but when you was inside the bank, how was it laid out?"

"They got grillwork in front like most banks, with places for two clerks behind the grills. Got them little openings where folks can make transactions with the clerks."

"Two clerks?" Henry asked.

"Yeah. Back a ways is where the banker sets. He's a feller with long hair and a wooden desk. His name is Blanding."

Buff nodded. "I met him at the barn. The liveryman said he's a nasty bastard."

Henry was not interested in personalities. "How about guns, Boice?"

"I didn't see any, but sure as hell they got them."

"Clerks or the head man don't wear them?"

"No, unless Blanding had one under his coat. I couldn't tell." Boice leaned back on his chair. "What I'd like to know is how much money they got in the bank. I knew a feller one time got caught robbin' a bank that only had sixty dollars. . . . He got six years. Ten dollars for every year."

Henry shifted his cud from one side of his face to the other. "No hurry," he told his companions. "Sooner or later there'll be a bullion coach along. Banks get money from the Denver mint an' other places. Boice, you keep your eyes open and let us know when a bullion coach is coming."

Boice nodded and eyed Henry, who he thought had a very good head for their line of work. They'd been active together one year, and Henry had always brought them off scot-free.

The singing drunk had either passed out or gone to sleep; they heard two men with spurs go down the hall and slam a door.

Boise arose and went to the window. "I got to get back. Them fellers at the corralyard bunkhouse know the saloon's closed. I won't be back in town for three days. This time I got to take a coach down to Edgerton. That's a long haul down an' a long haul back."

Buff and Henry watched the large man squeeze out the window. After he had disappeared in darkness, Buff closed the window.

Henry finally took two swallows from the bottle Boice had left, tossed his sucked-dry cud into the cuspidor behind the door, and went that far before turning to say, "Buff, keep the horses in good shape."

Brady nodded. "I got them in the biggest corral down there. They get plenty of exercise. I grain 'em every time old possum-belly goes over to the cafe."

"How about their shoes?"

"It wouldn't hurt to reshoe 'em, Henry."

"Fetch mine an' Boice's over tomorrow."

"What'll you tell Halderman? He'll know they don't belong to Ed."

Henry shrugged and reached for the doorknob. "Bring 'em over about noon when he goes up to the cafe. When he gets back I'll tell him some fellers come along and paid in advance. I'll give him the full price. All that old screwt thinks about is gettin' paid. I'll shoe them, an' you can lead them back over here. I'll do yours when the time is ripe."

Buff nodded, waited until the door had closed behind Henry, then sat down to kick out of his boots and get ready to bed down. When Henry brought the horses over he would have to tell the liveryman something, but since the animals had already been out back for a week, he wouldn't think much about it. Not Ed; he'd be thinking more about his britches always being at half mast.

CHAPTER FIVE

The Weather

BUFF WATCHED THE smithy. The moment he saw Halderman walking north toward the cafe, he led Henry's animal over, along with the big horse that belonged to Boice Candless. They did not exchange a word. Henry was ready and went to work as Buff crossed back to the livery barn.

It was one of those sultry springtime days with clouds and the scent of rain.

Ed Duval was at the cafe having lunch when Buff went over to get the freshly shod horses. Buff returned the shod horses to their corrals and was back sifting bedding into cleaned stalls when Ed Duval came down the runway, resplendent in a fine set of suspenders as red as blood. He ran both thumbs under them as he asked Buff how he liked the new braces. Buff laughed. "They can see you comin' from a mile off. Is that the only color they had?"

"No. They had some black ones an' some pink ones. Anythin' happen while I was gone?"

"No." There was no need to mention having the two corraled horses over to be reshod.

Buff was finishing spreading bedding when the first fat raindrops struck the roadway, causing tiny bursts of dust to rise. He went up front and breathed deeply. The sky was low and gray, heavy with water. The rainfall increased. Ed came up from the harness room to also sniff and watch. "They need it somewhere," he said over the increasing racket, "but not here in town."

For the full length of Main Street there was not a single person on the plankwalks, nor any horses at the tie-racks. In the wide opening that led into the stage company's corral-yard two men were hunched. As Buff watched, they retreated into the big palisaded yard, presumably seeking cover.

Ed Duval went back to the harness room and reappeared within moments, wearing a huge old hat. He said, "Be back directly," and went across the road to the far duckboards, heading for the saloon.

A tall, skinny man, wearing a black poncho that glistened from rainwater, came down to the smithy to lead freshly shod horses back to the corralyard. Buff watched him slither in the accumulating mud. It did not take much rain to turn Prairieton's roads into hog wallows.

Across the road Buff saw the blacksmith come to his door-way and scowl upward. Behind him someone—it had to be Henry—was warping steel over an anvil. Normally that sound would carry all over town, but now it was muted by the noise of the downpour.

Halderman turned back into his shop and removed his leather apron. There were no horses waiting to be shod, but there was plenty of other work. Replace spokes for a rancher's rig and rack up the shoes, according to size, that were made during slack time. There were pegs in the wall for that purpose.

Prairieton did as it usually did during a hard rainfall: it remained indoors as much as possible. Merchants did very little business, which allowed them time to arrange wares and do their ledger work.

The rain showed no sign of diminishing until late in the day, then it slackened off to a drizzle, by which time the roads were a mess, the corralyard had puddles, and about the only beneficiary of all this was Kent Overman. He had fired up his iron-cannon heater to keep the saloon dry, and tended his customers, most of whom had very little to say; they seemed to be waiting out the bad weather with poor grace but at least in agreeable surroundings.

Andy Collins and one of his yardmen, a large, pock-marked dark man, were at the bar, savoring drinks they really did not want. The emporium proprietor, with his impressive gold watch chain, buttoned vest and thin hair, was also up there, moodily hunched around a bottle and a little glass.

Someone broke the dour mood by noticing Ed Duval's fire-engine-red suspenders. "Fanciest set I ever seen," a local wag observed loudly enough to be heard above the drum-roll of rain on the saloon roof. "I once seen a lady up at Fort Laramie that wore somethin' like that to hold her stockings up. Same color, same sort of stretch. Ed, you sure you got a pair for holdin' up your *pants*?"

A clap of thunder rattled every bottle on the back bar and made the building shake. Several men went out front to look at the sky. It was still low and heavy and gray, not the kind of a sky that ordinarily brought thunder with it.

Across the road the banker was standing in his doorway, looking up. Behind him a man wearing a green eyeshade edged forward to also look out. Blanding turned on him with a snarl. The man with the eyeshade retreated from sight, and one of the men in the saloon doorway softly said, "Bastard," and turned back toward the bar.

Andy Collins, the stage company's local superintendent, worried aloud to the pockmarked man he was drinking with. "Damned roads'll be bad. We'll be lucky if any of the stages are within two hours of their schedule."

The man shrugged. "Nothin' a man can do about rain but wait it out." He carefully refilled his little glass, tipped his head back, and dropped the whiskey straight down. As he shoved the bottle toward his employer he also said, "Candless'll fish or cut bait this time. We'll find out how good he is tomorrow when he gets back."

"*If* he gets back," Andy said, looking at himself gloomily in the back-bar mirror.

His companion was not worried. "He'll get back. Like he told you, he's herded coaches before. The horses will be tucked up from pulling a coach with mud caked in the wheels, but he'll get back."

Andy wagged his head; his concern was for his coach, its hitch, and any passengers Boice might have picked up down at Edgerton. He knew from experience how bad the roads got when it rained hard.

Tony Halderman came in, stood in the doorway a moment shaking off water, then went directly to the bar without looking left or right. Kent brought a bottle and glass and walked back up the bar. He knew when Halderman was in one of his black moods and this was one of those times.

Ed Duval reset his huge old hat, snapped his red suspenders, and walked across the room, out through the spindle doors. He flinched as rainwater lashed at him. He remained as close as he could get to storefronts all the way down to the smithy. Down there he eyed the millrace in the roadway and started across. His boots were old and leaked. By the time he got to the bench outside his harness room they were full of muddy water.

Buff came in from forking feed out back. He too was wet. Ed's breath was cut off when he leaned over to pull his boots off. He had to wait briefly, take down a big breath, and tug again before he got them off. As he upended each boot, brown water ran out. He looked up at his dayman and had to raise his voice to express himself. "Any business?"

"No. Nothing."

Another thunderous roll came out of the sky. It made the old barn shake and frightened the corralled horses, who ran in circles.

Ed limped into his harness room, where rainfall always heightened the horse-sweat smell of blankets, collar pads, and saddle skirts. He poked his head out to ask if Buff had done the feeding. Buff had, so Ed said, "Quit for the day. No sense in settin' around here. See you in the morning."

Buff bypassed the saloon on the opposite side of the road as he hiked northward to the rooming house. He cleaned up out back, then headed for the cafe, which was almost full. The cafe also had its own unique aroma derived from man-sweat, greasy cooking, and strong tobacco smoke. The only topic of conversation was the force of the downpour, but inevitably someone could recall several much more forceful storms over the years.

As Buff was finishing his meal, Henry walked in. They barely exchanged a glance before Buff paid up and returned to the roadway. Now he was prepared to visit the Palace.

It too was crowded, but there was little conversation. The overhead racket pretty well precluded much talk.

Kent brought a bottle and glass, leaned over, and said loudly, "Ed told me you like the town an' might want to settle here."

Buff smiled. "It don't rain every day, does it?"

Someone striking the bar for service pulled Kent away. An older man with a badly lined and weathered face, standing next to Buff, said, "We'll take every drop that comes down." Buff looked at the older man; he had stockman written all over him.

Andy and his companion turned to leave, and someone called to him. "Hey, Andy, the good Lord don't have no use for stagers, didn't you know that?"

A ripple of rough laughter followed the men from the corralyard out into the night. They ducked their heads and plowed across to the corralyard, where Andy went to his office to light a lamp and do some work at the desk. His companion pushed back as far as the bunkhouse.

Buff went up to his room, shed his soggy attire, draped it to dry, and went to bed. It was late, at least he thought it was, and except for the local pool hall and the saloon there was not much in the way of recreation in Prairieton.

He was almost asleep when Henry rattled his door.

As Buff opened the door in his underwear, Henry said, "Boice is due back directly. I think I'd better do the special shoein' job on your horse tomorrow, an' then the three of us better do the job tomorrow when they're fixin' to close the bank for the day."

When Buff said nothing, Henry added, "I don't like leavin' over muddy countrysides but—"

"Give it another three, four days," Buff interjected. "Damned roads are too wet, an' there's a couple other things we got to figure out first."

"Like what? I'm gettin' tired of workin' for that old bastard at the smithy."

"Like we got to have it from Boice about things down at Edgerton. A lot rides on that, Henry."

"What else?"

"That's enough, mud an' not knowin' until Boice gets back. It was you, Henry, that said wasn't no reason for hurrying."

Henry Malden turned on his heels, went along to his own room, and disappeared inside.

Buff went back to bed but sleep did not come as easily this time. It did, eventually, arrive. In fact he slept right through until the silence outside awakened him. The storm had departed in the night.

Outside, Prairieton was wet inside and out, the roads were carved from runoff, and until the sun arrived later in the day, people would not begin to recover their spirits.

Buff got ready to head for the cafe. Henry had already gone down there, not actually motivated by Halderman's warning about not being late again, but because he was beginning to be restless. If it hadn't been for the damned rain he would have favored doing today what they had come here to do. Now they would have to wait for the ground to dry hard enough for horses to be able to make good time over it.

CHAPTER SIX
Fate Takes a Hand

ONE OF THE old gaffers who lived in the shacks at the lower end of town saw it first. He cackled until several other old men came out to stand like scarecrows staring southward.

One old man abruptly turned and went scuttling north-ward in the direction of the jailhouse. By the time he had breathlessly told Marshal Mosher, several other folks along Main Street had a sighting.

Will Mosher told the old man to go up to the corralyard and tell Andy, then he walked out front and stood, thumbs hooked in his shell belt, watching the stagecoach ap-proaching the lower end of town, the horses pulling it at a dead walk. Although the lines had been looped around the upright binder handle, there did not appear to be anyone on the box.

He started down there, but Ed Duval, who had been standing in his barn's wide front opening, was already moving to intercept the leaders. He had the coach stopped when Will Mosher got down there. Several old men gath-ered and Andy Collins approached with long strides. Other spectators were in the distance.

The coach was muddy, the horses tucked up and tired, and as Will Mosher approached one of the doors Buff Brady appeared. Opposite the livery barn Tony Halder-man and his hired man, Henry Malden, stood like statues.

Buff swarmed up the side of the rig, stopped when he could see the seat and the boot below it, and called down to the town marshal. "The driver's up here. There's blood all over. Get some help to lift him down."

Henry Malden left Halderman in the doorway, walked briskly forward, and as several strong men climbed up to lift the driver down, Henry spoke to Buff, who was still near the high seat. "Is he dead?"

Buff looked down, paused before replying because at least a dozen people were watching him, and finally said, "I don't know, but he's sure been shot."

They got Boice down from the high seat, which was no small accomplishment considering his size and his limpness. Will Mosher led the way to his jailhouse, down into the cell room, where Boice was placed on a bunk, and someone went for the local midwife, as near to a doctor as Prairieton had.

Mosher herded the spectators back as far as his office. Tony Halderman was standing there and did not move. He scowled fiercely at the town mashal and said, "Did you look inside?"

Mosher hadn't. He'd intended to, but Buff's shout had diverted him. "No. Anything in there?" he asked.

Halderman's long, thin upper lip lifted in a macabre smile. "A dead man. Shot square between the eyes."

"Get some fellers to help you and fetch him to the jailhouse." As Halderman turned away, Andy Collins pushed through. "What happened?" he asked. "There's blood all over the coach an' a dead man inside. The coach is heavy with mud but seems to be all right otherwise, but the horses—"

"Take it up to your yard, Andy. Take care of your horses an' don't let anybody near the coach. Not even your yardmen."

Even up as far as Kent Overman's saloon, clutches of people on both sides of the muddy roadway were busily talking. Steam was beginning to rise from the mud, the sun was hot and without any interference from drifting clouds, bore down hard.

Buff and Henry stood beside the cot, regarding their partner. Inert, unconscious and bloody, Boice had little color in his face. Marshal Mosher returned to the jailhouse and had barely got inside the little cell when a large, blowsy woman with gray-streaked hair and a little black satchel elbowed her way into the cell, and looked sharply at the lawman and the two men who were standing beside the cot. Without a word, she gave Buff and Henry a sharp elbow, leaned over the bloody, unconscious large man, and said something under her breath.

She opened her satchel, removed some shears, and went to work cutting away Boice's shirt. She called for a basin and hot water; the lawman left to get them. During his absence the big woman spoke to Buff and Henry without looking up from her work. "I been patching folks up for thirty years. Mostly deliverin' babies, but bullet holes too, and knife cuts along with busted arms an' legs, but this one here, I don't know. He bled out real hard. One of you take the shell belt and gun off him."

Henry moved forward to obey, and as he stepped back with the shell belt draped over one arm he lifted out Boice's six-gun, opened the trapdoor, spun the cylinder slowly, closed the little door, and sniffed the barrel. Without a word he handed the weapon to Buff Brady, who made the same study of it before dropping the weapon back into its holster.

There were two unfired cartridges in the gun. Four empty casings indicated that the gun had been fired four times.

The midwife straightened up, drying her hands on a clean, threadbare towel from her satchel. She stood gazing at the unconscious man as she said, "Must have been quite a scrap. He got hit three times, once alongside the ribs between his side an' the inside of his arm, which don't amount to much, once through the fleshy part of his upper right leg, and again in the back, but that one must have come from a considerable distance because I can pop the slug out."

Henry and Buff looked relieved. "Nothing worse?" one of them asked. The woman turned like a she-bear.

"Nothing worse? He bled all over the place. You can get a bullet in the butt, an' if the bleedin's not stopped, you can die."

She turned her back on Henry and Buff and went back to work. Will Mosher arrived with a jug of hot water and a chipped white enamel basin that he put on a chair and set it close by the midwife. She did not acknowledge his return until she moved one bloody hand and something metallic fell into the basin. She resumed washing the wounded man, and despite his size and heft, she eased him onto his side and back as though were a child.

Will Mosher looked at the bloody cloth on the floor. "A lot of blood, Mabel."

Her response was typical. "What could you expect, Marshal. He's been shot three times."

"What are his chances?"

She replied to that as though, having had the same question asked so often, she could reply by rote.

"He's breathing. As long as he can do that I'd say that even bled out like he is, he's got a fair chance. I don't know, Marshal, any more than you do. Does he have a room somewhere?"

"At the corralyard bunkhouse," Mosher replied.

"He can't stay there. Have you ever seen inside that shelter? It's filthy and smells to high heaven."

Henry broke in. "He can get a room up at the hotel. Be easier for you to keep an eye on him up there."

The midwife did not respond. She had washed the wounds, dosed them with carbolic acid, and was now bandaging them. When she straightened up to rinse off in the basin's pinkish water, she looked at Marshal Mosher. "Nothing more you can do here, Marshal Mosher, if you want to circulate around an' see what you can figure why someone shot him."

Mosher pointed to the cell opposite, where the dead man from inside the coach had been carried.

The large woman snapped her satchel closed and followed her guide into the opposite cell. This time she did not open the satchel as she made an examination, but she surprised Will Mosher by freeing a money belt from inside the dead man's clothing and holding it back for Mosher to take. She went back to her examination without a word, but when she finished she emptied the dead man's pockets and placed the items beside him on the cot.

Her only comment as she stood gazing down was "Much too young to die. Shot through the head. Never knew what hit him. Well, if you get that other one settled in up at the rooming house let me know. He's going to need care for a while yet. Unless he lost too much blood, in which case he'll be dead by tomorrow. I'll come back in an hour or so to see how he's doing. Good day, Marshal."

Mosher almost forgot to answer, but he did. "Good day to you, Mabel. We're all real obliged to you."

At the door the woman's hard gaze went over to Mosher. "I got a cellar full of 'Much Obliges.' Can't get a dime for 'em."

The marshal handed over two cartwheels, and the midwife departed.

Marshal Mosher returned to the opposite cell, watched Boice's chest barely rise and fall, then faced Buff and Henry with the money belt in his hands.

"I recognize the dead man." Mosher held out two folded dodgers, each describing a pair of highwaymen who worked together. "This one's Clark Malone. Works with a partner named Paul Runyon."

Buff and Henry read the records of Malone and

Runyon; they were wanted in such widely divergent places as Idaho and Texas. Their specialty was robbing bullion coaches. Their last assault on a coach was south of Denver. They shot a gun guard that time. Their haul was a crate of newly minted greenbacks destined for a bank down at Bridgerton near the Colorado–New Mexico line.

Blanding stamped into the office up front and bellowed for Marshal Mosher, who turned on his heel, still carrying the money belt, and hastened up front. Buff looked at Henry, who spoke bitterly in a low voice. "We're goin' to be hung up in this damned town for two months, maybe more." He was about to say more when a loud voice caught and held their attention from the direction of the jailhouse office.

Marshal Mosher sounded more surprised than angry when he said, "What? Without gun guards, for chrissake?"

"Gun guards," the loud and furious jailhouse visitor exclaimed. "No one was supposed to know. If I'd hired guards down there it'd have been the same as tellin' the world a strongbox of money was on that damned stage. Will, I want that box back. The strength of the bank depends on it. You understand?"

"One of 'em is in a cell, dead. He had this belt under his britches. I know their names. The one in the cell was Clark Malone. His partner's name—"

"I don't give a damn about that," the banker exclaimed. "I want that strongbox. You get up a posse and find that other one, the son of a bitch who made off with it."

The town marshal explained about the coach driver being wounded and lying on a bunk in one of his cells. He started to explain about the extent of the injuries, but the banker cut him off.

"Get your damned horse, get some possemen, and find that man with my strongbox. I don't give a damn who got shot and who didn't. I want that money. You understand?

Go run him down if it takes a month. Don't come back without the money."

A door slammed so hard the rugged building shook. Henry went to lean on the wall and fish for his plug. As he was doing this he said, "This beginnin' to make sense to you, Buff?"

Buff nodded while eyeing the unconscious man on the cot. "Yeah. Boice was bringing a money box to the bank up here. Knowin' Boice, I'd say he was happy as could be, because now there wouldn't be no doubt about the Prairieton bank havin' lots of money."

Henry cheeked his cud and made a wintry smile. "To Boice that was our money an' he put up a hell of a fight to keep it . . . Buff, we better ride with the marshal's posse."

Neither of them made any effort to inform their employers they would ride with Marshal Mosher's posse, but since the rallying point was the livery barn, where several possemen had to get horses, Ed Duval saw his dayman rig out his own animal and leave town on the south trace, along with Henry and two others, one of whom was big Will Mosher.

Ed Duval crossed to the smithy to tell Halderman his hired man, as well as Ed's, had gone out with the posse. Oddly enough, Halderman did not explode. But neither did he act very pleased. Whatever else people thought of him, Halderman was a strong supporter of law and order.

Ed was walking back to his runway when the Prairieton midwife caught him and asked if he had any laudanum.

He took her to his harness room, dug out a small bottle, and spoke as he handed it over. "You sure he'll make it?"

The reply was cryptic. "I wouldn't bet my life on it, but I think so. Be more sure tomorrow if he's still around."

Ed watched the large woman walk toward the jailhouse. A few minutes later some raggedy-pantsed rangemen turned in out front, and since Ed had no dayman to care for their animals he had to do it himself.

At the jailhouse Boice Candless was beard-stubbled and gimlet-eyed. As soon as he regained consciousness, he asked for water. The midwife got it, helped him drink, and had to get a refill and hold him until he'd drained that one too.

As she eased him back down he asked where the town marshal was. Her reply was curt. "Gone with a posse."

"Which way'd they go?"

"South. That's the way you come into town slumped down in front of the box, the hitch pokin' along on loose lines."

"You know the fellers who rode with the marshal?"

"There's Paul Lincoln from the corralyard, an' two fellers I don't know, except that I've seen 'em. One is the liveryman's day hostler, the other is the town blacksmith's helper. I don't know their names, but they look capable enough."

Mabel leaned down to change the bandages and pursed her lips a couple of times; there was swelling and discoloration, but where she'd expected to find high fever, there was none. She used the back of one hand to brush graying hair off her face as she said, "You hungry?"

Boice said he was thirsty, not hungry. When the midwife finished treating and bandaging the wounds she went after some water into which she tipped a dram of whiskey from the marshal's desk drawer.

Boice drank and did not once take his eyes off the large woman until the glass was empty and he was flat out again. Then he said, "What's your name?"

"Mabel Foster. What's yours?"

"Boice Candless. How long am I goin' to be down?"

Mabel pursed her lips. "I don't like to answer questions like that. My specialty's deliverin' babies. Women come to me and think by pokin' their bellies I can say when the nipper's due. In your case it'll take time for the wounds to heal, but you lost a lot of blood. You might be able to walk again directly, when you get enough strength to try it."

"How long, lady!"

"A month. Three weeks anyway, an' if you get an infection you could damn well die." Mabel took the basin out back and flung its contents into the alley, returned, and dried her hands while eyeing Boice Candless. "You got a bed at the corralyard bunkhouse?"

"Yes."

"Well, you better stay right here. Less chance of catchin' an' infection. I been in that boar's nest up there. Now I got to go look after my regular trade, but I'll be back this afternoon, or maybe a little later."

Mabel nearly collided with Jeremy Blanding in the doorway. They exchanged minimal nods and the banker stepped away to let Mabel pass, then went down to the cell occupied by Boice Candless and stood looking down.

Boice was drowsy, but he looked straight back. There were no preliminaries to their conversation. Blanding wanted to know what happened and why Boice had allowed one of the highwaymen to get away with the strongbox.

Boice's black eyes showed nothing as he replied. "I don't know much of what happened after the shootin' commenced. I saw 'em ride out of some timber on the east side of the road. They both had carbines aimed straight at me."

"So you threw down the box."

Boice ignored the interruption. "I waited until they were riding toward the coach where I stopped it, then I dropped down into the front boot, drew, and shot at 'em. One managed to climb into the stage, but I shot him before he could reach me.

"That other one was as fast as greased lightning. He couldn't see me down in the boot, but he knew I was there. He spaced his shots to hit me no matter whether he could see me or not."

"You didn't get a shot at him?"

Boice's gaze at the banker hardened. "Mister, I didn't know anything until I woke up with some lady workin' over me."

"Then you didn't see him get the box, nor which way he went?"

"I just told you, after I got hit I must have passed out. I don't remember anything."

Blanding stormed out of the cell and out of the jailhouse. Andy Collins, walking toward the jailhouse to visit his driver, passed the banker, who did not even look in his direction. Andy paused in the jailhouse doorway to watch the banker turn into his brick building, then wagged his head and went down into the cell room.

Boice was soundly sleeping.

Andy returned to the office, sat on the wall bench for a while, then returned to his corralyard.

Most of the excitement had passed. There were still a few people standing around talking, but for the most part Prairieton's recent shock had greatly diminished.

CHAPTER SEVEN

Runyon

THERE WERE TRACKS all the way down to where the highwaymen had stopped the coach, easily distinguishable from other wheeled vehicles by the width of the steel tires.

They found a saddled horse east of the road, where feed was tall. Despite the bit in his mouth, he grazed along until he saw the four riders over in the road, then he threw up his head, ready to run if he had to.

Will Mosher ignored the horse. They could catch it on their way back. Right now he wanted the tracks of the lone surviving highwayman who had the strongbox.

The lanky corralyard man, Paul Lincoln, quartered. As Henry and Buff watched, it became clear why the town marshal had brought Lincoln along. He was an accomplished sign reader.

He was a hundred or so yards easterly when he stood in his stirrups and whistled, then flagged with his hat. Will Mosher led the way. Lincoln was gnawing a corner off a fresh plug when the others arrived. He gestured with one arm.

The tracks were there, plain as day. When Lincoln had his cud tucked, he said, "Sort of southeast." He sat a moment, sprayed amber, then addressed the town marshal. "Marshal, just how full was that strongbox?"

Mosher had no idea. "Why?"

"Well, if it was paper money we might have a fair ride ahead, but if it was metal, maybe silver an' gold, it's got to be pretty heavy, an' a man ridin' a horse balancin' that thing can't go very fast."

They followed the tracks for an hour, until the marshal was satisfied they were not going to change course, then he led his companions in a long lope parallel to the highwayman's sign, but a hundred yards east of it.

The countryside was gullied in places, timbered in other places, and pure grassland for as far as a man could see in other places.

They rode, alternately watching the countryside and occasionally returning to the tracks to be certain their bandit hadn't altered course.

He hadn't.

The sun climbed, and its heat combined with the humidity made the ride a sweaty, debilitating event.

Will Mosher had been trying to guess how much time had been lost since the stage returned and he left town with his possemen. It was important, because if he knew that, he could come fairly close to guessing how many miles ahead their outlaw would be.

Henry rode back with Buff. His interest had nothing at all to do with elapsed time. Henry was a very practical man; they were on the trail of the outlaw, and his sign was abundantly clear. All they had to do was continue to ride until they had a sighting, or until they tracked him to a hiding place.

The idea that crossed Buff Brady's mind was very different. He had little doubt of the outcome of this pursuit. What intrigued him was that he and Henry Malden were riding with the law on a manhunt.

The corralyard man loped ahead, then was lost to sight by his companions when he dipped down into a wide arroyo. Even after he emerged on the far side, there were trees that shadowed his progress until he was deep within the timber. Marshal Mosher dropped back to ride with Buff and Henry.

Lincoln had come back out of the trees and was facing across that wide arroyo. He neither called aloud nor signaled; he just sat there.

This time it was Henry who led the way down into and across that arroyo. When he came up into the trees, Paul Lincoln was standing loosely beside his horse. He waited for the marshal and Buff before saying, "There's an old couple got a few goats, chickens, and whatnot up ahead about a mile. His tracks go straight toward that place."

Will Mosher asked if the old couple had horses. Lincoln shrugged. "One old gray buggy mare, born about the same year I was. He wouldn't take her. You ready?"

Lincoln turned back into the trees and led them out the far side, where they saw the house, small barn, and fenced garden patch. They heard the chickens before they saw the coop and runway.

Runyon's tracks went arrow-straight toward the little, weathered house where a white-headed man was standing on the small front porch with a Winchester hooked in one arm.

Paul Lincoln rode out front with his right arm in the air, palm forward. Behind the old man a woman stood framed in a window with a long-barreled shotgun in her hands.

Henry smiled at Buff. "Be interestin' to hear how the highwayman made out, eh?"

They rode up to the tie-rack in front of the house and halted. They made no move to dismount. The old man was lined and noticeably arthritic when he moved. He recognized the town marshal and spoke without any preliminaries. "You're about three hours behind him, Marshal. He come up on us from out back. We didn't know he was out there until the chickens commenced squawkin' like they do when they smell coyotes. He bought a sack of food an' rode on." The old man leaned his weapon aside, fished a greenback from a pocket, and held it up. "Brand, spankin' new.

Never even been creased. My wife says it's either counter-feit or that feller robbed a store or something."

Henry asked about the condition of the man's horse. The old man eyed Henry as he replied. "It's been rode a spell, but it's one of them buckskins that're tougher'n rawhide."

"Did he say where he'd come from or where he was heading?" Mosher asked, and got a faint frown from the old man before he answered.

"All he said was he'd pay for a bundle of grub. That's all. No thank-you, nice-day, or nothin'. He stood with the horse until my wife made up the bundle an' I took it out to him. He took it, handed me that twenty-dollar note, got astride, and rode off southward. That's the whole story from start to finish."

Lincoln said, "Three hours? Hell, Marshal, he could get down to Edgerton ahead of us."

Without comment, Will Mosher dismounted to water his horse. The others did the same. The old man leaned his carbine aside and approached the town marshal to ask who his visitor had been and what he had done. When Mosher told him, he returned to the porch and spoke to his wife through the window.

They left the isolated little homestead, quartering for sign; when they found it, Will Mosher had Lincoln lope ahead. He thought Runyon would head for Edgerton, and if this was correct, Runyon's tracks would begin bearing more westerly soon.

Lincoln came back and confirmed the lawman's guess. The three of them headed back toward the stage road, where they could make better time.

Henry shook his head at Buff; unless something delayed the fleeing outlaw, he would reach Edgerton well ahead of the posse riders.

Buff called ahead to the marshal. When Mosher looked

back, Buff said, "The old man didn't mention a strongbox."

Mosher nodded. He hadn't asked, but the old man would have told them if the fleeing man had been carrying one. He was confident Runyon had shot the box open somewhere back yonder, stuffed its contents inside his saddlebags, and hid the box.

When they had a solid roadbed underfoot, they picked up the gait and held to it for quite a while. They would have held to it longer, but a range rider on the east side of the road stood in his stirrups and waved his hat. He was near a stand of second-growth pines.

Will Mosher sent Henry to find out what the man had signaled about. Mosher, Lincoln, and Buff Brady continued southward, but at a slow walk.

Henry met the rangeman north of the pines. The man was agitated and his words tumbled forth all run together. He pointed in the direction of the trees. Henry only understood about half of what the man said, but when the cowboy turned to lead the way, Henry followed.

Ten minutes later Henry came out of the trees facing the roadway, fired his six-gun into the air, and beckoned with his hat.

Mosher led the rush toward the trees where Henry waited. There was no sign of the rangeman. Henry did not say a word; as the cowboy had done, he turned his horse and led the way through the pines to a small, grassy clearing where a tired horse was listlessly cropping grass, too tired to even show interest when other horses came into the clearing. The saddlebags on both sides of the cantle in back looked stuffed almost full, their gullets were distended, but no one paid attention to the horse or the saddle on his back.

The rangeman was squatting beside something bulky in the tall grass. He looked up as Buff, Lincoln, and Mosher appeared, then got stiffly to his feet.

Henry hung back as the lawman and Paul Lincoln walked ahead. He caught Buff's arm and softly said, "Dead. I'd guess one of Boice's shots hit him too, only not hard enough for him to go down until he got this far."

They walked up to where the others were standing, looking solemnly at the dead man. Marshal Mosher stooped and flopped the corpse over. They all saw the patch of blood. The dead man had been hit high on the right side. There was no exiting wound, the bullet had evidently struck bone and had lodged in it.

Lincoln said, "Bled out inside."

Marshal Mosher asked the rangeman how he'd happened to find the dead man. The cowboy told him he'd been hunting strays, saw fresh tracks in the soft earth, and ridden among the pines to this place. He had not seen the body in the tall grass until after he'd seen the ridden-down horse.

Marshal Mosher approached the saddled horse, and Buff and Henry went over to hold the horse while the lawman unbuckled the near-side saddlebag. Mosher looked in, went around the off-side without saying a word, and did the same thing again. He rebuckled the bags and leaned across the listless horse's back, looking at Henry and Buff. "Greenbacks," he said. "Looks like a fortune. I figured it had to be paper money when he ditched the strongbox." Mosher stepped away from the horse. "Ten more miles or thereabouts and he'd have got down to Edgerton. If he took a train down there, chances are real slim we'd ever have heard of him again."

Paul Lincoln had walked over in time to hear the last thing Will Mosher said. He spat, ran a soiled sleeve across his lips, and eyed the town marshal. "Mister Blanding gets his money back. I hope he chokes on it."

The rangeman left them. He had wanted to leave even before he saw them coming down the road. Finding a dead man could be more trouble than a man needed.

Though he was a large, powerful man, Marshal Mosher had to get help hoisting the limp corpse across the saddle. He said it was like trying to hoist a sack of wet sand.

When they were ready to leave the little clearing, Mosher gave Henry the highwayman's saddle gun, gave Buff his shell belt and holstered Colt, and told Paul Lincoln he could have the man's rig but not his horse. The horse, once it had been fed up and rested, would be auctioned off to reimburse Prairieton for the expense of burying its owner. That had been the custom since the founding of most towns west of the Missouri River.

They took their time returning. There were a number of things to think about on the way back, not the least of which was the bluntly offered physical evidence— bumping along belly-down across his tired horse—that crime did not pay. At least for the outlaw partnership of two men named Clark Malone and Paul Runyon.

Henry had once told Buff there was reason to believe that crime *did* pay. The reason folks said it didn't pay was because successful criminals did not announce to the world what the source of their wealth was.

The southbound stage from Prairieton passed them at a dead walk, passengers and driver craning to watch the four possemen and their dead companion pass by.

Paul Lincoln offered his plug around, got a cud tucked into his own cheek, and said, "How much money did Mister Blanding say was stole?"

Will Mosher had never heard the exact amount. "I got no idea, but from the amount stuffed into them saddle-bags it was a lot."

Lincoln rode a hundred yards before speaking again. "Might be a good idea to count it, Marshal."

"Why? Runyon didn't get a chance to spend any of it."

Lincoln spat aside before replying. "I know a little about Mister Blanding. If I was in your boots I'd make sure how much we got before turning it over to him."

Buff and Henry regarded the lanky man thoughtfully, but Marshal Mosher did not act as though he'd even heard.

By the time they had rooftops in sight, Runyon's horse was clearly failing. They slackened to a shuffling walk in order to keep the animal going until they reached the alley behind Ed Duval's barn. Once there, they carried the corpse inside, placed it faceup in an empty stall, and went back to care for their animals.

Buff put the Runyon horse in a stall, grained and hayed it, and waited until the other animals had been looked after and Mosher and Lincoln had left before jerking his head at Henry.

They went through the dead man's pockets, not expecting to find much, and at least in this they were not disappointed. They were sitting on the bench across the runway when Ed Duval walked in. He had been up at the saloon. If people had seen the posse riders return, and surely some had, none met Ed to tell him.

He nodded to Buff and Henry, went down the runway to see if the stalled animals had been fed, found only one, a ridden-down, listless animal that had, and turned to the opposite stalls. Buff and Henry heard him gasp. He was leaning on the door of the stall with the dead man in it, staring straight up from drying eyes.

Henry shoved up to his feet, tapped Buff on the shoulder, and walked toward the roadway.

Ed turned slowly, eyes wide. He said, "Is that the other one?"

Buff nodded.

"Well, he can't stay in there. Go tell the marshal to get him the hell out of my barn. It's bad for business."

Buff remained seated and regarded the fat man. "It's your barn, Mister Duval. You tell him."

Ed stood briefly, then went lumbering toward the roadway on his way up to the jailhouse. Buff stood up, stretched, took down a hayfork, and went about doing the chores. Then he stood in the doorway of the harness room, looking at the Runyon saddle from which Marshal Mosher had removed the saddlebags. He returned to the stall where the dead body was stiffening, removed the man's shell belt and holster, took them back to the harness room, and hung them from a peg.

Across the road Henry was washing up at the quenching tub, answering questions put to him by Tony Halderman. His answers were cryptic. When he finished washing, Henry said he was hungry and walked past Halderman on his way to the cafe.

The blacksmith watched him depart and for once did not snarl or even scowl.

Buff and Henry met in front of the cafe. They no longer minded being seen together since they had ridden with the posse. Buff wanted to see Boice, but they entered the cafe first. The cafeman raised enquiring eyebrows. Neither Buff nor Henry volunteered anything except their orders for a meal.

Other diners eyed them but, taking their cue from the treatment they had given the cafeman, said nothing.

Paul Lincoln came along. He too had washed. As he sank down beside Buff and called his order to the cafeman, he sighed and shook his head. "That son of a bitch," he said quietly. Both Buff and Henry looked at him.

Lincoln explained. "Mister Blanding heard we was back an' was waitin' at the jailhouse when the marshal walked in. He demanded the money be counted, so Mosher counted it." Lincoln paused until the cafeman had put down his cup of coffee and departed, then said the rest of it. "That son of a bitch said the count come up two hunnert dollars shy."

The cafeman arrived with three platters that he noisily placed before the possemen and stamped back in the direction of his cooking area, clearly in a bad mood. But none of the three possemen noticed as Lincoln spoke again.

"There was a big argument. Mosher said it all had to be there because Runyon hadn't had time to spend any of it, an' Blanding said he had the invoice from the bank down at Edgerton and what he had counted in the marshal's office was two hunnert dollars shy.

"The marshal hit the ceiling. He said Mister Blanding was sayin' him or one of us that rode with him stole the money, and he could swear none of us even looked into the saddlebags but him, an' if Mister Blanding was accusing him, he'd better come right out an' say it, and the marshal would break his neck. He also told Mister Blanding you two fellers an' me went after his damned money, took the risk, and the least he could do was thank us."

Henry said, "And?"

"That was the end of it, Mister Blanding left the jailhouse with his money in Runyon's saddlebags, madder'n a hornet."

Buff asked how Lincoln knew all this. The stage company's yardman answered while picking up his eating utensils.

"I went down there to remind the marshal he give me Runyon's outfit. I had in mind takin' it up to the yard an' maybe sellin' it to Andy. I was outside when the shoutin' started. I sat on the bench out front until Mister Mosher left. He didn't even see me settin' there."

After they had eaten, Paul Lincoln departed and Buff led Henry outside before saying, "You suppose Runyon cached two hundred dollars on his ride south?"

Henry snorted. "He was shot. If you was shot would you think about hidin' part of the money? Neither would I."

"Then what happened to the two hundred dollars?"

CHAPTER EIGHT
The Daydream Fades

HENRY AND BUFF got a surprise over at the jailhouse. Marshal Mosher told them Boice Candless had been moved, on order of the midwife, up to a clean, airy room at the hotel.

He also told them of his run-in with the banker. They had already heard about it, but they listened politely anyway because the marshal was still furious and had to let off steam.

When they got to the rooming house the moody proprietor was on the porch. He looked up irritably when they asked where Boice was. "He's in room number eight. It ain't locked. That old witch is in there with him. If I'd ever thought about marryin', bein' around her for fifteen minutes would have cured me."

They heard the midwife before they got up to room number eight. Mabel was raising hell because someone had snuck a pony of brandy to Boice.

When they walked in, she turned on them. Buff offered his most disarming smile; Henry went over beside the bed. Boice winked and Henry winked back.

The midwife was rolling clean bandaging cloth to put into her satchel and had her back to the men, but when she was finished she turned and said, "If you're friends of his maybe you can talk sense into his thick skull. Any kind of liquor is bad for someone in his condition." She snapped the satchel closed and stormed out of the room.

Henry and Buff waited a moment, during which Boice

said he had given Dougherty, the rooming-house owner, money to get him whiskey at the saloon, and the old screwt had returned with brandy that burned like fire because, he avowed, brandy was better medicine than whiskey.

Buff was pleased to see Boice looking well, still a little peaked around the eyes and mouth, but otherwise vastly improved over the last time he had seen him.

Henry, though, was solemn. On the ride back with Runyon and the town marshal he had thought hard about something he did not like at all. He said, "Boice, you're goin' to be laid up for a month. That money we got back for the bank is in there right now. If we wait around for you to get well, the lord knows how much will still be in there."

Boice and Buff gazed at Henry. They understood the implication perfectly. Boice said, "Like hell. Give me a week an I'll be ready to ride."

Henry said nothing, but they knew that no one as shot up and bled out like Boice Candless was would be ready to ride in a week. He'd be damned lucky if he could walk as far as the livery barn in a month.

Henry went to stand by the window that looked southward through town. Buff, feeling uncomfortable, pulled up the only chair and straddled it. Boice watched Henry, then swung his attention to Buff. He looked disagreeably suspicious. "You ain't figurin' to do the job an' leave me here, are you? Hell, Buff, it was me that braced them two highwaymen for that strongbox."

Henry turned. "I been tryin' to figure out a way to get you out of Prairieton. You can't set a horse, an' settin' up in a stage over that washboard road would be just as bad." He walked over to the bed. "Leavin' you behind would be best, but we partnered together too long for Buff'n me to do that, even though I'm sure you'd be safe. They couldn't even suspect you, Boice, you bein' flat on your back and all."

Buff seemed to think the idea of leaving Boice was better the way Henry explained it, but it was obvious Boice Candless did not share that notion. He lay there looking at Henry until Henry said, "Well, it don't have to be decided right this minute. That money'll be there tomorrow an' most likely the next day." He smiled thinly. "Think on it, Boice. Think of some way we can move you. You too, Buff. Good night, see you tomorrow."

After Henry's departure Boice stared moodily at the door Henry had closed behind himself. "How about a dray wagon with straw on the bed an' maybe a couple of blankets. You could get one from Duval," he said to Buff.

Buff nodded about getting the rig, since that was not the problem nor was the fact that since they would not return it, Ed Duval would have to hire someone to go down to Edgerton to fetch it back. The problem, as Buff saw it, was loading Boice into the wagonbed and driving south with him after raiding the Prairieton bank. It didn't make a lick of sense. Marshal Mosher and most likely half the damned town would scour the countryside.

Any way Buff looked at it, Boice had made it possible for the bank money to be recovered, at the price of being seriously wounded. So far as that went, it was fine, but by getting himself shot up he had just about destroyed the careful planning that had gone into their preparations for the Prairieton raid.

Later, when he was back in his own room, Buff had another, even more unpleasant, thought. If they abandoned Boice, made their raid, and escaped, as he was certain they would do, an abandoned Boice Candless probably would spill the beans to Marshal Mosher.

Buff and Henry might still escape, but if Boice told the entire story, they would probably have an unwelcome welcoming committee waiting for them at their final destination.

Buff lay in bed a solid hour, gazing at the ceiling. Their

original scheme, which they had worked out over several weeks of leisurely riding on their way down to Prairieton, had been the best he had ever heard of. He had been keeping busy at Duval's barn, thinking about a future in which he had plenty of money. He had daydreamed about a number of choices: buying a cow outfit or a saloon in a prosperous town, or maybe taking the steam trains back East to see places he'd heard about since childhood. Maybe even settling down with a wife and just loafing for a few years.

Henry had told them several times around the campfire that this was going to be their best, probably their last, chance to become rich men. That had kept Buff's and Boice's spirits high during the long, often dreary ride south from the Montana countryside where they had met while riding for a big cow outfit.

When an occasional misgiving had arisen, as they were bound to do on that long a ride south, Henry had patiently explained everything again, even drawing diagrams in the dirt.

By the time they had got into the Pawnee Valley country, they knew precisely what each of them was to do, and they had accomplished everything according to plan, right up to the moment Boice had got himself shot up doing his damnedest to ensure the Prairieton bank would be full of money.

The following morning after breakfast, Buff arrived at the livery barn in a taciturn, gloomy mood. To Ed Duval, who had only known his dayman to be pleasant, conscientious, and knowledgeable, the change was instantly noticeable. But he asked no questions.

Across the road Henry matched his employer in long silences, something the blacksmith did not notice until the day was well advanced and a pair of out-of-town stockmen rode up and tied their horses at the rack.

Halderman looked over to where Henry was working, oblivious to the customers out front. Halderman went out himself.

He knew both stockmen. They said they'd be in town until evening and would call back for their horses later. Halderman led the animals inside, dumped their riding equipment on the earthen floor, and called to Henry, who was pumping the bellows.

Henry did not even look up until Halderman came to the rear doorway.

"You gettin' deef?" Halderman asked. "I said them two horses want shoeing. Their owners'll be back directly. They're cowmen from southwest of town. Got a long ride ahead of 'em without havin' to wait around for their horses."

Henry turned slowly, regarded the blacksmith, and without a word, shouldered past him to get the first horse. He cross-tied it and went to work. Halderman remained in the rear doorway, watching. When Henry neither looked his way nor spoke, the blacksmith went forward, pitched his apron across an anvil, and went hiking toward the saloon. He was convinced something was bothering his hired man and hoped to high heaven it wasn't something that would require Henry to quit him.

On the way toward the Palace he saw the local midwife entering the rooming house. Halderman continued toward the saloon.

When Mabel opened the door, Boice eyed her arrival stoically. He respected her talent, even approved of most of what she said and did, but he did not like her.

She pulled the blankets back and, without a word, snipped the bandaging away. She was gentle at this, but when the wounds were exposed she examined them with something less than concern for the pain she caused.

Boice bore it without complaint. She was very thorough. When she straightened up, she smiled. Boice was so surprised he forgot the pain. "No infection," she announced, as though it were a miracle, and maybe it was. "Your clothes were dirty, everything around you was dirty. I would have bet when I came around today you'd have pus sores."

Boice watched her soak a rag with carbolic acid and locked his jaw. She returned to work without looking at his face. "They are going to heal. There will be scars. You can't expect anything different when you get shot. Years ago they brought me a man who had been shot in the face. His jawbone was busted on both sides and he'd been lying on the ground a while before anyone thought to carry him down to my house. He was filthy."

"He lived?"

"Yes, through the grace of God, although I never could imagine why God would bother with such a worthless person. Anyway, he healed. It took a year, an' his lower face healed crooked. He had to learn to eat all over again an' he didn't sound right when he talked, but he lived."

"How did you fix a busted jawbone?"

The midwife did not answer until she had finished cleaning the wounds and stepped back to survey her work. Then she answered offhandedly. "All I did was get as much of the bones together from inside his mouth as best I could, then made a cast for the inside and the outside of his face, an' kept him on his back so's I could mind him an' feed him with a little spoon."

She looked at Boice. "He was the worst patient I ever had."

"He should have been grateful," Boice muttered.

"He was. By the time he left we couldn't stand the sight of each other. I never figured to see him again. One night three years later he rode up out front; it was a hot summer evening. I was settin' out on the porch. He didn't even dismount. He flung a little buckskin pouch to me and rode off without a word. There was three hunnert dollars in gold in the pouch."

"Was he a rangeman?" Boice asked dryly.

"No, Mister Candless. He was an outlaw. I saw his picture on a wanted dodger right after he left."

Boice nodded slightly and Mabel made her final remark about that episode in her life. "I patch folks up an' deliver live babies when I can. I don't set in judgment on anybody. I never told the marshal about the dodger or the three hunnert dollars. I did my best for him, an' three years later he rode by an' done his best for me. Now then, roll up onto your side an' don't talk."

Boice rolled onto his side and gazed thoughtfully at the wall. When she finished and told him to lie on his back, he had made up his mind about something; it might take a while but he would do it.

When the midwife was finished and had closed her satchel she cocked her head at him and asked a question.

"Why did you take on three-to-one odds to save Mister Blanding's money? You could have been killed. In fact you damned near were. Why, Mister Candless?"

Boice's gaze slid away from the woman's face as he fumbled for a believable answer. "Well, I take it personal when someone tries to rob my coach."

The midwife put a pitying look on Boice as she picked up her satchel and started for the door. She spoke as she was opening the door and without looking back.

"Most graveyards got fools in them. Some of them are about your age."

She closed the door after herself and Boice smiled mirthlessly at the door.

CHAPTER NINE

Boice's Dilemma

MARSHAL MOSHER ENTERED the saloon, saw Buff and Henry, and bellied up beside Henry at the bar. He settled in, nodded to Kent Overman for a bottle and a glass, then turned to regard Henry for a moment before speaking.

"What happened to Tony? I was just down there an' he was passed out like a rock."

"A horse he was shoeing kicked him on the knee," Henry explained. "He's all right, but I got him a bottle to shut him up. He was groaning like a bear with a sore behind."

Mosher nodded when Kent brought his bottle and glass, offered to refill Henry's and Buff's glasses, and as he was pouring, Mosher said, "Someday, mark my words, someday it won't be a horse. I've seen him light into a few fellers. If the darned fool don't learn to control his temper, someday he's goin' to cross the wrong person and get shot." After downing his drink the marshal asked who was going to run the smithy if Halderman couldn't get around.

Henry smiled as he lifted his jolt glass. "I got no idea. He fired me because I wouldn't let him shoot the horse."

Will Mosher's brow dropped in a scowl. "You've lasted longer than most. He's not goin' to just up and hire someone; folks around Prairieton know him too well. Even the qualified ones won't work for the old devil."

Henry was studying his raised glass when he replied. "I'll show up in the morning. If he fires me again, I'll quit. If he don't. I'll run things until he can get around . . . The damned fool."

After the town had gone to bed Buff and Henry visited Boice again.

"According to Mabel the midwife, Blanding didn't thank anyone for gettin' his money back," Boice said.

Buff shrugged about that. "From what folks say, he wouldn't thank the angel Gabriel for holdin' the gate for him." Buff looked at Henry. "Ed Duval told me today that was Blanding's personal money, not the bank's."

Both Henry and Boice scowled. Buff made a little gesture with both hands. "That's what he told me. I got no idea whether it's true or not."

As Buff and Henry were ready to depart, Boice had a question for them. "Suppose we hired a special wagon to haul me down to Edgerton in the next couple of days? The midwife said they got a real doctor down there. I could get her to say I need a professional pill roller or I might die. I'd already be down there when you fellers come along."

Buff smiled at Boice. "That's pretty good. You figure that out by yourself?"

Boice scowled. "You think only you'n Henry can come up with something?"

Before Buff could reply, Henry had a question for Boice. "Did you sound her out about this?"

Boice hadn't; he'd only had the thought when he awakened from his nap. "No, I didn't."

"What makes you think she'd do it?"

Boice's reply was brusque. "She told me about patchin' up a feller who got shot in the face, an' he passed through one night and gave her three hunnert dollars." Boice paused before telling them the rest of it. "She saw a dodger on him an' never told the marshal."

Henry nodded thoughtfully. "Try it," he told Boice, and went to the door. "Be careful what you say to her. We'll meet again tomorrow night."

Out in the dingy corridor Henry stood a moment facing Buff as though he had something to say, but instead of speaking, he gave the younger man a slight pat on the shoulder and walked toward his room. As he was bedding down it occurred to him that after months of careful planning for the Prairieton raid, first Boice got shot, then that cranky old bastard he worked for got kicked in the knee, and while he considered Halderman and his damned injury more of an annoyance than an obstacle, he went to bed in a gloomy mood. Fate it seemed was creating delays. His original idea had been for the three of them to settle in, work in the community until they were familiar with it—something he had envisioned requiring no more than a couple of weeks—then make their raid and disappear. The town marshal, the whole damned town for that matter, would never find them.

The following morning he was as solemn as an owl when he arose. He cleaned up, went down to the cafe, and from there he went down to the smithy. The wide front doors were open, exactly as he had left them the previous evening.

He did not look into the sooty little cubbyhole of an office, but pumped life into the forge and tied his apron into place. He was examining the wheel he'd been working on before Halderman got kicked when Marshal Mosher walked in and called a cheerful "Good morning." Henry returned the greeting, but not as cheerfully.

Mosher looked for something to sit on and remained standing. A blacksmith shop had soot everywhere. In an old shop like this one, everything a man touched left his hands spotty with the stuff.

He watched Henry testing the wheel to be sure the tire and rim had melded, before he said, "Tony's sicker'n a dog. I went round to his cabin below town to check on him. Mabel the midwife visited him last night, told him she wasn't comin' back until he took an all-over bath, gave him a pinch of laudanum, and refused to even look at his leg."

Henry nodded at this and asked if the marshal had looked at the leg. Mosher had. "It's swelled up dang near as big as a small flour sack. He can't put any weight on it. Between havin' the grandaddy of all hangovers an' worryin' about the shop, he told me to hunt you up and tell you you was hired back at least until he could get around. My guess is that the cranky old screwt won't be able to put weight on that leg for a month."

"That disagreeable old son of—"

Mosher interrupted. "I know all that. I've known him a lot longer'n you have. I also know somethin' else. Between forge work and shoein', this shop is the only one in a hell of a long day's travel where professional blacksmithin' is done. I can guess how you feel about Tony, but if you'll stay on, I'll have a talk with him."

Henry showed a tight little smile. "Fair enough, Marshal," and as the lawman returned to the roadway Henry shook his head and went back to work. If Halderman would be unable to run the shop for a month, by the time he returned, Henry and his companions would be long gone.

Shortly before noon Ed Duval brought over a horse he had just traded for. The big horse was fairly young and had no collar sores, so evidently he hadn't been used a lot.

As they stood looking at the big horse, Henry said, "You can come after him about closing time."

Ed tucked both thumbs under his red braces. "How's Tony?" he asked. All he wanted was to be reassured that someone would continue to operate the shop. He did a steady business over there.

After Henry told him he would be looking after the place for a while, Ed went back to the livery. When his dayman came in, Ed told him that the new feller Halderman had hired was running the smithy.

Buff returned to the runway and across the alley to the

wagon shed, a long, three-sided building. Ed Duval had two top buggies in there, three dray wagons, one belly-dump wagon, and a pair of light spring wagons.

Buff looked closely at the two spring wagons. If Boice was hauled south down to Edgerton it would have to be in this kind of a rig. It could be filled with bedding, and because this kind of rig had springs, the jolting would be minimal.

Buff and Henry did not meet until Ed asked Buff to go over yonder and fetch back that big workhorse.

Henry was finishing the rasping when Buff arrived. Buff sat on the up-ended horsehoe keg until Henry was finished and slowly straightened up as Henry reached around to untie his apron.

Henry sleeved sweat off, gave the big horse an affection- ate pat on the rump, and said, "The marshal said it could be a month before Halderman will be back here." Henry smiled. "Ought to be quite a backlog of work piled up by then with no one to do it."

Buff was not especially interested. "Ed's got the rig to haul Boice down yonder. Good springs under it, fairly new, an' tomorrow I'll pull the wheels an' grease every- thing."

Henry looked sardonic. "Depends on the midwife, Buff. If she agrees he needs professional care down yonder, then I figure you'n me can make the raid maybe day after tomorrow. Give Boice time to get down there well ahead of us."

Brady took the big horse back across the road where Ed Duval leaned over as far as he could to check the shoes and grunted back upright, looking pleased. "Put him out back in a corral. That helper of Halderman's is a better shoer than Tony is. I hope he don't quit like the others."

Buff did not say a word. He led the big horse out back, closed a corral gate on him, and returned to the wagon shed to consider which of the spring wagons was the best.

Day after tomorrow wasn't very far away.

CHAPTER TEN

The Wheels Are Turning

THE FOLLOWING MORNING Ed Duval went outside and stopped dead in his tracks. His dayman had one of the spring wagons blocked up, with all four wheels off. He was slathering grease, and as Ed looked, Buff held up a ragged grease retainer. "Worn through, Mister Duval."

Ed nodded. "I got some in the harness room," he said, and went back up the runway, shaking his head. He'd never had such a conscientious hired man before. In fact he'd never even heard of one that conscientious. He took the retainer out back and leaned in silence, watching the younger man work until someone bellowing up front diverted him.

Jeremy Blanding stood wide-legged with hands on his hips, and as usual he was curt.

"Need my rig," he told Ed. "Now!"

Ed nodded and scurried after the vehicle. As he pulled it inside and went after Blanding's big mare to be backed between the shafts, he said, "Goin' to be a hot day, Mister Blanding."

The banker did not reply. He sat on the bench impatiently. When Ed grunted in exertion as he bent over to straighten the harness, Blanding finally said, "Why don't you shed fifty, sixty pounds? Directly you're going to be so fat you'll waddle."

Ed reddened, worked in silence until the rig was ready, then turned with a forced smile and said, "I'm goin' to do that, Mister Blanding," and stood in the middle of the runway as the banker led his rig out front before he climbed in. Ed's stare was venomous. He returned to the alley, where Buff was tightening the wheel bolts. Ed helped his dayman push the rig back inside the shed and said, "That was the banker, that miserable son of a bitch."

Buff picked up a rag to wipe his hands. "Haven't heard very much good said about him, Mister Duval."

"An' you never will. There's a cowman west of town named Chester Grant. He's had a bad couple of years. A few weeks back he tried to get a loan to tide him over, and Blanding turned him down."

Buff shrugged. "They got to be careful when they're managin' other folks' money, don't they?"

Ed showed worn teeth in a bitter smile. "You know about that money them two dead highwaymen stole? Well, that was Mister Blanding's own money. He had it in the bank down at Edgerton. He needed it because he's foreclosing on Chet Grant."

Buff looked blank.

Ed looked annoyed. "You don't understand? He needed that money to bid on Chet Grant's ranch when the foreclosure is completed."

Buff, who knew nothing about foreclosures, looked at the older man. "So he'll own the ranch?"

"Yes. An' the cattle, an' everything on the ranch. Nice feller, eh?"

"Why don't that cowman go down to the bank at Edgerton? They might make him a loan."

Ed rolled his eyes. "Partner, the bank down there'd get in touch with Blanding. He'd tell 'em not to, but even if he didn't do that, they most likely wouldn't make a loan to someone from up here. It'd be out of their territory."

The sound of horsemen caused the liveryman and his hostler to go back inside. Out front at the tie-rack two tired-looking men were leaning beside their animals. From their appearance, they'd been on the road quite a spell. Ed talked to them as Buff took their horses down the runway to be cared for. Later, Ed returned to say the strangers had asked him the name of the local lawman and where he could be found. This information had no immediate, visible effect on Buff, but when Ed went into his harness-room office, Buff decided to take a second look at the horses he had just corraled.

He had noticed the brands; they had struck him as familiar, but he hadn't paid much attention. The second time he looked at them, he had misgivings. The horses belonged to a cow outfit in northern Montana. He had seen the brand a number of times before. In fact the ranch those horses came from adjoined the ranch he, Boice, and Henry had ridden for.

Under normal circumstances this would have been of normal interest, but to Buff Brady these were not normal circumstances.

He did not return to the runway, but went around the corrals and hiked briskly over to the blacksmith shop.

Henry listened and made a reasonable judgment. He, Buff, and Boice had robbed a stage and a general store before heading south. Henry doubted that their crimes in Montana were of sufficient magnitude for possemen or lawmen to ride all the way down to Pawnee Valley in pursuit. But a man could never be certain. He told Buff he'd find an excuse to talk to Marshal Mosher, and Buff went back across to the livery barn.

It was midafternoon before Henry strolled up to the saloon. Marshal Mosher was not there. Kent said he'd ridden south early in the morning. Henry and Kent had a pleasant conversation until some freighters walked in and Kent went to take care of them.

Henry returned to the shop. Between jobs he watched the roadway for the marshal's return, but as things turned out, those two Montana riders had to have their animals

reshod, and they appeared at the shop just short of supper time.

Henry also recognized the brands on their horses. The
strangers spent a few minutes at the shop. The last thing
they said before heading for the cafe was that they'd be
back for their horses about dusk; they had a long ride
ahead of them and would like to make the next town before morning.

Henry watched them head for the cafe before going to
work on their horses. It was impossible to tell whether they
recognized Henry from a dodger or not, but his impression was that they had not. It was even possible that no
dodgers had been made of the three men.

Still, Henry's certainty that they had to complete their
raid and be on their way was heightened by the appearance
of the men.

Later, when he was hanging up his apron for the day, the
pair of strangers walked in. Henry nodded and led them to
where their horses had been corralled. One of the strangers, a thin man with reddish stubble, paid for the shoeing
job with silver. His companion, shorter, darker, and un-
smiling, paid in paper. It was this forbidding-looking individual who said that in case the blacksmith saw the local
marshal, he might tell him that two lawmen from Montana
had passed through.

Henry agreed to tell Will Mosher, and stood in the shop
doorway, breathing a deep sigh of relief.

He went to the cafe for supper, expecting to see Buff at
the counter. There was no sign of him, even though Henry
dawdled over a third cup of coffee.

Dusk came late, and full nightfall did not arrive for another hour or so, by which time Henry had cleaned up and
was sitting in his room when someone ran his knuckles
across the door.

Buff walked in, looking freshly shaved. As Henry was
closing the door, Buff asked about the Montana lawmen.

Henry told him what he knew, and asked if Will Mosher had returned to town.

He hadn't. If he had, Buff would have known because the town marshal kept his horse at Duval's barn, and that, coupled with the appearance of the Montana lawman, had Buff worried.

Henry did nothing to ease the younger man's anxiety. "We got to do it no later than the evenin' of the day after tomorrow. Now, let's go see what Boice's got to say."

Henry knocked once and was reaching to open Boice's door when the door opened inward. Dougherty stepped back for them to enter and tossed a remark at the man in the bed on his way out.

"Don't let that old witch know, Mister Candless."

Boice agreed. "I won't." After the door was closed, Boice held up a pony of whiskey, which explained the hotel proprietor's presence and his last remark.

Buff bushed the Dougherty episode aside. He asked if Boice had talked to the midwife. Boice nodded and offered them a drink from the bottle, which they both declined.

"She said I was comin' along fine. She said as far as she could see, there wasn't no call for me to go down to Edgerton to their sawbones. She said it was up to me, but she wouldn't advise makin' that forty-mile trip, because it'd probably bust things open."

Henry pulled a chair around and straddled it before telling Boice about the Montana lawmen. Boice looked at them both before saying, "That's cuttin' it a little close to home, ain't it? If they seen dodgers on us . . . Buff, can you get a team an' a wagon?"

Buff nodded. "I'll fill it with hay an' blankets."

Henry asked dryly who was going to drive. Boice thought he probably could, but Henry shook his head slowly.

Buff had the answer. "I'll drive. I'll tell Ed that Boice's

got to see the doctor down yonder and hired me'n the spring wagon."

Henry sighed. Forty miles down and forty miles back would take two days. The raid would have to be postponed another day, until Buff got back. For a while there was silence. Eventually Henry spelled it out for them, but neither Boice nor Brady seemed troubled. Henry had to be resigned, but those Montana lawmen had made him uneasy. As he arose from the chair he said, "All right. Figure it so's you'll be back before evenin' of the day after tomorrow."

Brady nodded. "I'll start back as soon as I got Boice settled in down there. Drive all night if I got to."

He did even better than that. The next morning he left a note for Ed Duval, explaining his absence with the spring wagon, loaded Boice atop layers of hay and blankets, left town before any lights showed, and was well on his way some time before dawn, with Boice wrapped like a cocoon.

Henry was having breakfast when Ed Duval came in, sat down beside him, gave his order to the cafeman, then said, "That feller that got shot hired my dayman to haul him down to Edgerton to the doctor."

Henry chewed, swallowed, and was reaching for his coffee cup when he replied. "He was pretty bad off, Mister Duval. A medicine man's trained to look after wounds like he got."

Ed was willing to believe that, although he had worlds of faith in the midwife.

Later, when Henry was down at the shop firing up the forge, Marshal Mosher walked up.

Henry told him about the pair of Montana lawmen passing through. Mosher shrugged; it was customary for lawmen to call on local authorities when they were in a town.

"Goin' south, were they?" Mosher asked.

"North," Henry replied, easing up on the bellows because the coke in the forge was pale red. "I shod their horses. They said they wanted to reach the next town north before dawn today."

"Must have been in a hell of a hurry, or maybe on a trail."

Henry nodded without speaking. He was still a little spooked by those Montanans.

Mosher finally got around to the cause of his visit. "I sat with Tony for a spell last night. That leg of his looks like hell." Mosher paused as Henry shoved a bar of steel into the forge, occasionally turning it. "Something he said might interest you."

Henry raised the bar. It was white hot. He took it to an anvil to be warped half around into the rough shape of a plate horseshoe.

Mosher watched; one thing was a pure fact. Halderman's helper was experienced at his work. The marshal waited until Henry had cut the formed shoe loose from the rest of the steel bar and shoved the bar back into the forge. Before Henry could start beating the pale steel into a shoe the marshal said, "Tony's gettin' a little age on him."

Henry looked ruefully at the cooling steel, left it atop the anvil, and faced the marshal. "He does pretty good, Marshal. I've worked with blacksmiths older'n he is."

"Maybe, but that knee's goin' to bother him a long time. It'll be a while before he can put weight on it, so he asked me to come see you."

"About what?"

"Selling out to you."

Henry turned back to hammer the cooling steel. For a while the noise inhibited any further conversation. The shoe had cooled too fast. Henry lifted it with tongs and pushed it back into the forge. He also withdrew the blank bar and cinched it in a vice. Clearly, he was not going to be able to continue his work for a while. He gave the bellows a couple of hefty pumps before facing the marshal again.

"It's a little late," he said. "Few years back I'd have jumped at the chance of ownin' a shop."

The marshal hooked both thumbs in his shell belt. "You're good at your work. A man who knows his trade as well as you do should be workin' for himself. He didn't set no figure, but in his condition I'm pretty sure you can work something out."

Henry fished for his plug, cheeked a cud, and shook his head. "I'll think about it, Marshal."

After Will Mosher's departure Henry did think about it, with chagrin, because he had wanted to own his own smithy for several years, but working for rider's wages, he had never been able to put aside enough money.

He went back to work and was not interrupted again until late afternoon when Jeremy Blanding walked in out of the fading sunlight. Henry nodded as he removed his apron.

Blanding forced a smile and got directly to his reason for being there. "Halderman wants to sell out. Around town they say you're the best forgeman that's ever come to Prairieton. I'm in the business of making loans. Banks thrive on the interest they make off secure loans. If you want to buy Halderman out, come see me."

Henry had not said a word and did not say one now as the banker strode back out into the roadway, moving as a man might who had just visited a place where a person dared not sit down because everything was dingy and smelled of brimstone.

Henry spat into the forge's cooling coals. He'd bet new money the town marshal had talked to the banker.

He spent the balance of the day making two sets of flat plate shoes. After punching holes in each shoe, he held them at arm's length to study them, then placed them separate from the other new shoes. He then closed up for the day.

At the Palace saloon the town marshal again brought up the possible buyout, and as before, Henry said he would think about it.

After Henry left to go up to the hotel to clean up, Marshal Mosher told Kent Overman the new blacksmith sure wasn't talkative.

Overman, who'd had several pleasant conversations with Henry, did not think that was true. But all he said to Will Mosher was that maybe Henry had something on his mind.

For a fact Henry did have something on his mind. After making himself presentable he went down to the bank. It was a little short of closing time, but when Jeremy Blanding saw Henry, he came forward from his desk and opened a little gate.

He pointed to a chair beside his desk, sat down, leaned back with both hands folded over his stomach, and said, "You give it some thought, did you?"

Henry nodded as he looked around. "Yeah. Depends on how much Mister Halderman wants and how much I can borrow to buy him out. . . . You got a nice bank here, Mister Blanding."

The banker rocked forward. "We do all right," he replied, and gestured toward two cubbyholes behind a grillwork where a pair of clerks sat on high stools caring for customers.

There was a massive steel safe facing into the room. It was very noticeable; in fact, everything Henry saw left him with the impression that the bank had been arranged to impress people.

Blanding glanced at a gold watch, pocketed it, and said, "It's closing time. If you come back tomorrow we can talk. Have you got a figure from Halderman yet?"

"No, sir."

Blanding liked the subservient tone. As he arose and shrugged into the coat that had been on the back of his chair, he said, "Do that. Go see him tonight. Get his lowest figure and come see me tomorrow. All right?"

Henry arose. "All right."

As he walked toward the roadway door a clerk followed, and as soon as Henry was outside, the clerk slammed the big door.

CHAPTER ELEVEN

Ready!

AFTER SUPPER HENRY went down to the shacks at the lower end of Prairieton, knocked on a door that had four up-turned horseshoes nailed on it, and when a voice he recognized called crankily that the damned door wasn't locked, Henry entered.

There was one window in the room. It was on the north side, where precious little light could ever come through. Tony Halderman was sitting in a rocking chair with his injured leg straight out, resting on another chair. The furnishings were meager; the place looked, and smelled, like it hadn't been cleaned in a long time.

Halderman pointed to a little stool, but Henry remained standing. Halderman said, "Well, you must have talked to Will Mosher."

Henry replied that he had and looked for another chair. There were only two and Halderman was using both.

Halderman looked at his helper through narrowed eyes. "An' you come to horse-trade." Grudgingly the blacksmith gestured toward a dented small coffeepot atop a cluttered woodstove. "Coffee, if you want it. Can't lace it. That danged midwife took my bottle."

Henry regarded the bandaged knee. "What did she say?"

Halderman cleared his throat before replying. "She said—an' that dang woman's pure mean all the way through—she said the kneecap was cracked an' some tendons behind it was maybe either punched sideways or busted, an' if they're tore loose, when the damned thing eventually heals I'll likely, at the best, always have a limp, an' at the worst, if they don't ever heal, I'll have to use crutches."

Henry tried to be reassuring. "She could be wrong. I've been kicked on the knee and got over it, but it took a while."

Halderman gave Malden a gimlet-eyed glare. "But you're a lot younger'n I am."

Henry gave it up. The Angel Gabriel could fly through the door to reassure Halderman and he'd tell him to mind his own business and clear out.

"Make me an offer," Halderman said abruptly.

Henry's reply was typical of anyone who had ever traded horses. "I can't sell your shop an' buy it too, Mister Halderman. It's yours, you put a price on it."

"You been to see Blanding?"

"Briefly, it was closing time at the bank."

Halderman relaxed and stared in the direction of the cluttered stove. When next he spoke, his tone of voice was almost civil. "Henry, see if you can borrow the money somewhere around town. Maybe from Overman, but not from Jeremy Blanding if you can help it."

"I don't know that many folks around town, Mister Halderman. All I can do is ask the price, an' either take it or leave it. If I take it, I got to go to the banker."

"You'll regret it to your dyin' day."

"Maybe—how much?"

"I built that forge myself. I paid good money for three of them anvils. I gave an old man who's dead now sixty dollars for the property. He'd used it for a tannery for years; the smell an' flies was so bad in summertime . . . well, you're as good a forgeman as I ever knew. Can you stand three hunnert dollars? Remember, Henry, there ain't another smithy within miles. You're gettin' a goin' business with all the trade you'll be able to handle."

Henry didn't dicker. The only reason he had come down here was to have a valid reason for going back to the bank. Probably not tomorrow, because Buff wouldn't be back, but the day after, with Buff, just at closing time.

"I'll let you know in a couple of days," he told Halderman and turned toward the door.

Halderman stopped him with a hand on the latch. "I been thinkin' since I talked to Will Mosher. There's another way we can work this. You take over the shop an' pay me a percentage of the business. That sound fair to you?"

Henry did not say whether it sounded fair or not. He opened the door as he said, "I'll let you know in a couple of days."

"Wait a minute—you been runnin' the shop since I been crippled. The money you've took in is rightly mine. I pay you wages."

Henry smiled a little. "I'll give you an accounting when I'm ready. Hope that knee mends."

He closed the door, took in a deep breath of fresh air, and considered the advance of dusk. By now Buff and Boice should be down yonder.

He went up to the saloon, which had a fair-sized crowd, and got a bottle and a jolt glass that he took to a distant table.

There had been a day when he'd have bought the shop if he'd had to go to the devil for the money.

Will Mosher ambled over and sat down uninvited. Henry pushed the bottle and jolt glass toward him. Mosher ignored them. "You talk to Tony?"

"Yep. He wants three hundred dollars for the whole works."

Mosher nodded. "That's not too much. He likely took in twenty, thirty dollars a day durin' the summer season."

Henry watched the lawman tip the jolt glass full. "I don't have three hundred dollars."

"Try the bank."

Henry waited until the marshal had downed his whiskey before speaking again. "I did. I'm supposed to see Mr. Blanding tomorrow."

Will Mosher was so confident of the outcome of their forthcoming meeting that he turned to another topic. "It's good country, Henry. It'll grow. A man could do a lot worse than to settle here." Mosher pushed the bottle and glass toward Malden, got more comfortable, and also said, "You know that feller who rode with us when we found that dead highwayman?"

"Paul Lincoln?"

"Yeah. He's goin' to quit the corralyard an' hire on with me as a deputy." At the look he got from Henry, Mosher added a little more. "Springtime's passing, and when summer comes, rangemen comin' to town from all the ranches can keep two men busy, specially on weekends. More trail traffic lately too, and settlers stakin' claims along the foothills. Like I said, Prairieton's growing."

What Henry particularly remembered about the lanky corralyard hostler was that he was a good tracker. But he only nodded in agreement with what the marshal had just said without mentioning Lincoln's particular talent.

But it was something to think about, and later, on his way to his room at the hotel, he thought seriously about it. By now, the ground was almost completely dry after the earlier storm.

When he was back in his room, standing at the window, he smiled. This was what he had planned for. Not Paul Lincoln, the tracker. But someone. There were always trackers after a raid.

The following morning, as he was tying his apron into place, he saw the banker's top buggy go whirling northward from Ed Duval's barn, which meant there would be no point in visiting the bank until Blanding returned to town.

It was a busy morning. He had to weld a broken strut

for the stage company and pull four sets of shoes for Ed, who was going to turn some horses out to pasture. By the time he saw the top buggy pass on its way back to the livery barn he was ready to take a little time off.

He shed his apron, washed, and took his time arriving at the bank. Jeremy Blanding was at his desk and looked up with a nod as Henry appeared at the little gate.

Blanding pointed to the chair beside his desk, but did not smile or offer his hand. Rocking back in his chair, he said, "Good thing you didn't come earlier. I had to leave town for a couple hours. Got a foreclosure comin' up."

Henry nodded without comment.

"Did you talk to Halderman?"

"Last evening. He wants three hundred dollars for the property an' the business."

Blanding eyed Henry. "It's a good business. The bank'll loan you two hundred dollars."

"I need three hundred, Mister Blanding."

"Got no money of your own, eh? You got a horse an' saddle? They might bring a hundred." Henry was getting red in the face; Blanding knew all the signs, he'd seen them dozens of times before. He rocked forward with both arms atop the desk. "Bank's got to be careful. Suppose I loaned you the full three hundred an' you saddled up and rode off with it? I'd be out three hundred dollars an' I'd have a blacksmith shop on my hands. You see? If you got a real close interest in it, you'll stay an' work hard."

Henry's gaze wandered. Blanding had seen that before, too. "Two hundred. I'll have the note drawn up. You can come back this afternoon, sign it, an' get the money. Halderman might come down if you show him two hundred in greenbacks." The banker arose. "This afternoon."

Henry took his time leaving the building. Both the clerks in their little cubbyholes looked at him and looked quickly away.

There were four or five people in the bank. Henry recognized Andy Collins from the corralyard and Dougherty from the rooming house; they both nodded and he nodded back.

Outside in the sunlight he saw Ed Duval taking a horse from a traveler in front of his barn. The traveler had matching britches and coat, plus a stiff-brimmed, low-crowned black hat. He could have been a circuit judge or a preacher.

Down at the shop Henry put on his leather shoeing apron, waited until he saw Duval heading for the cafe, then crossed over and brought two horses back to the shop with him. One belonged to Buff Brady, the other one was his own animal. He left Boice's horse in the corral with the other horses. Boice wouldn't need him.

He corraled the horses behind the shop and was returning when the stranger entered. The man was weathered, with a beak of a nose and close-spaced gray eyes. He told Henry he wanted his animal shod and that he could find it across at the livery barn.

Henry nodded, and said he'd have the horse ready in an hour or so. When the stranger asked him where he might find the local lawman, Henry told him, then stood in the doorway watching the stranger hike northward to the cafe.

The two horses he'd corralled could wait. He did not intend to shoe them until he saw Buff return.

When he crossed the road, Ed Duval was leaning in the barn door, sucking his teeth. Henry told him why he was there and Ed grunted himself up and led the way to a stall. As Ed led the horse out, he said, "Sixteen hands if he's an inch. Belongs to a feller they call the Manhunter."

Henry took the lead rope. "Dresses more like a preacher. You know him?"

"Don't really know him, but he's been here before. He's a bounty hunter. Got a hell of a reputation. Cousin of mine up north at Colorado Springs was there when this feller snuck up on some horse thieves durin' a blizzard. They was playin' poker in a log house a fair distance from town with a fire goin'. He got right up to the only winder and shot all four of them settin' at the table playin' cards."

Henry's brow dropped. "No warning?"

"In his business they don't give warnings."

"What's his name?"

"I never asked, an' he never said. Did you talk to him?"

"No. He said he wanted his horse shod. I agreed to do it. That's all. Except that he asked where he could find the marshal."

Ed's eyes narrowed. "Then, sure as we're standin' here, he's on a trail."

Henry returned to the smithy with the tall horse, cross-tied him, and stood back. The big horse was either pure thoroughbred or at least three-quarters thoroughbred.

He went to work pulling the worn shoes and preparing the hooves for the new set. As he was doing this he ran several possibilities through his mind, each of which had to do with ways of temporarily laming a horse.

In the end, he used none of them; chances were that the eagle-beaked man in black was not on the trail of three men who had robbed a store and a stage way up north. His kind hunted down men upon whose heads there was a sizable reward.

But Henry's normal calm was a little troubled. This was the second time men had appeared in Prairieton whose trade was finding outlaws.

When he finished with the big horse, he took him back to his stall across the road. There was no sign of Ed Duval. Out back across the alley two men were talking. Henry recognized both voices. One was Ed Duval; the other, Buff Brady.

He ambled to the back and watched Buff and the livery-man push the spring wagon back to its place in the shed. They did not see Henry as Buff handed four silver dollars to Duval. "He paid me down there, Mister Duval."

Ed pocketed the money and smiled. Henry walked into the alley, ignored Buff, and told Ed he'd put the bounty hunter's horse back in his stall; from the corner of his eye he caught Buff's expression.

Henry turned on his heel and went back to the shop to get the pair of special shoes he'd made. He was considering them from the viewpoint of a professional horseshoer when Buff arrived. He hadn't shaved and should have been tired from his recent long drive down yonder and back, but he did not act tired as he said, "Ed told me about that bounty hunter. Henry, I think—"

"How tired are you?"

"I left Edgerton right after I got Boice settled at the hotel down there, an' slept most of the way back. The team never left the road. I'm hungry but—"

"Go get fed, Buff. Take your time. I got to shoe the horses an' the bank don't close until just short of sundown."

Buff hesitated as though he wanted to say more, but Henry was already on his way to bring in their horses.

At the cafe Will Mosher sat down next to Buff and asked how the stage driver had stood the trip to Edgerton.

"Bled a little around a couple of places where scabs was forming, otherwise he did right well."

"What did the doctor down there say?" the marshal asked.

Buff had not seen Edgerton's medical man. "Said he'd look at him when he had the time."

The cafeman came, they ordered supper, and Marshal Mosher responded to greetings from a couple of townsmen who came in and hunkered down at the counter.

Buff tried to think of some way to casually mention the bounty hunter. He did not have to; as Marshal Mosher looked at the platter the cafeman set in front of him, he said, "There was a train robbery at a place called Ford's

Crossing, about sixty miles southeast of here. Four fellers got off with six mail sacks and a strongbox."

"When?"

"Three, four days ago. There's a feller on their trail. Feller named Loosely." Will Mosher picked up his knife and fork. "He's called the Manhunter. He was in town today, needed new shoes on his horse. He's goin' to lie over tonight, then take up the trail tomorrow. I never cared much for him—he's been here a few times before. As cold-blooded as a damned rattlesnake."

Buff ate most of his supper and drank three cups of coffee. After he paid up he debated whether or not to return to the smithy and tell Henry what he had learned.

In the end he went to the rooming house, pocketed his razor and his few belongings, then headed to the blacksmith's shop, with the sun reddening as it began to descend toward the faraway rims and peaks.

Henry had completed shoeing one horse and had the second one, Buff's animal, cross-tied and half-shod when Buff walked in. Henry looked up, nodded, and went back to work. With two nails in his mouth he said, "We got about an hour. You all right?"

Buff wasn't all right any more than he'd been all right when they stopped the stage up north or when they had robbed that store; but he nodded and told Henry what he had learned about the bounty hunter.

Henry said nothing until he had the last shoe nailed and was twisting off the nail ends. "One thing we got to do, Buff. Take two of Duval's horses, bridle 'em cheek to cheek with about a foot of slack, and on our way south, we'll hooraw them northward in a dead run."

Buff understood, waited until Henry was straightening up from the shoeing, then asked, "Suppose someone up there pulls a gun?"

Henry studied his shoeing job as he replied, "Shoot him."

CHAPTER TWELVE

Getting the Job Done

BUFF CROSSED THE road and sat on a bench where he could watch the smithy and the bank. He rolled and lit a smoke.

Henry finished the few things he had to do at the shop, stuffed some money into a little brown paper sack, and cleaned up.

It was close to supper time, and the roadway had very little traffic. Shoppers and dawdlers were gone from both sides, some storekeepers were trundling in the wares they displayed in front on the plankwalks. A late stage entered town at a dead walk, traces slack, horses ready for what they knew would happen once they were unharnessed; a bait of hay, a good roll in corral dust.

Henry sauntered across the road to ask if Buff had picked out the pair of horses to be cheeked for the run northward.

Buff arose from the bench, emulating Henry's casual attitude. "Yeah, they're in the last two stalls on the north side. If Ed's at the cafe we'll have no trouble."

Henry nodded. "Let's go."

They walked without haste, reaching the bank as the midwife emerged carrying a money pouch. She nodded to them and walked past.

One of the clerks appeared in the doorway, prepared to close up. Henry smiled at him, "It'll only take a minute. I got to see Mister Blanding."

The clerk looked unhappy, but he stepped aside as they entered, then closed the door behind them.

Jeremy Blanding already had his coat on and was talking to the other clerk, a gray-faced, chinless man whose watery eyes blinked as Blanding berated him for something.

Blanding turned, saw Henry and Buff, and said spitefully, "The bank's closed. Come back tomorrow. Henry, I can't make that loan for more'n a hundred and fifty dollars."

Henry smiled as he approached the little gate, shoved it open with his knee, and looked back at where Buff and the other clerk were standing. Buff nodded almost imperceptibly.

Henry faced the banker again, still smiling as he drew his six-gun without haste and cocked it.

It was so quiet in the bank with the roadway door closed that when the clerk beside Buff gasped, they all heard it.

Henry wigwagged his cocked Colt. "Open the safe, Mister Blanding."

For a few seconds the silence lingered. No one moved.

Henry moved closer to the banker and his terrified clerk, and repeated it. "Open the safe!"

Blanding found his voice and blustered. "Are you crazy? You'll get ten years in the penitentiary."

Henry's reply was dead calm. "We'll risk it. For the last time, open the safe."

Blanding got red in the face. He had a revolver in his desk, but the desk was ten feet behind him. "Henry, listen to me—"

"We don't have the time, Mister Blanding." Henry turned his attention to the ashen-faced clerk. "Mister, hand me that pillow you sit on. The one on your stool."

The clerk was baffled. "My pillow . . . ?"

"Yes."

The clerk got off his stool and handed Henry the pillow. Henry held it in front of his six-gun and moved to within six or eight feet of the banker. "Are you goin' to open the safe, Mister Blanding? They won't hear the shot in the roadway."

Blanding's color remained high. His mind was working fast: he had to cause as much of a delay as possible. He said, "I got the combination on a piece of paper in my desk."

Henry nodded. "Get it . . . If you got a gun in there, leave it. You couldn't lift it, cock it, an' aim it before I blow your head off. . . . Get the paper. Use your left hand in the drawer, Mister Blanding."

The banker moved grudgingly to his desk. The clerk beside Buff fainted. Buff stepped away as the man fell. Henry did not take his eyes off Blanding. "The drawer," he said quietly, moving a little closer.

Blanding looked down at the desk, his jaw muscles rippling. He opened the top drawer with his left hand and took a slip of paper from the drawer. The gun was loaded and ready. He stared at it as Henry said, "Close the drawer!"

Blanding obeyed.

Henry jerked his head. "Go open it, Blanding, we're wasting time. I'm going to kill you if you don't stop dawdling."

Sweating, Blanding approached the large steel safe, then looked over his shoulder. Henry stepped close, tossed the pillow aside, and jammed his gun barrel into Blanding's back. The banker flinched, leaned slightly, and began turning the large combination knob. As he twisted it the last time he said, "Henry, for chrissake—!"

"Open the door and shut up!"

Blanding had to step aside as he swung the door open. Henry gave him a shove forward. The banker halted, looked back at Buff and his cocked gun, and spoke again, his voice sounding higher this time. "They'll run you down like a rabid wolf, Henry."

Henry was filling a white cloth sack with banded stacks of greenbacks, paying no attention to anything else. He opened several drawers and emptied them too. When he had cleaned out the safe, he knotted the top of the sack and closed the safe's heavy door.

Someone knocked loudly on the front door. For a moment Blanding's expression reflected hope, but the hammering stopped. Buff, standing near the door, used a sleeve to push sweat off his face.

Henry gestured with his six-gun. "On the floor, Blanding."

As the banker obeyed, Henry nodded to Buff, who told the watery-eyed clerk to come from behind his cage and also lie on the floor.

They lashed all three men, using belts and in Jeremy Blanding's case a necktie. They then ripped cloth from the curtains and gagged them as well. Henry went over each prisoner very closely. When he was satisfied, he tossed the white sack to Buff and told him to empty the cash drawers. While Buff was doing this, Henry sank to one knee beside the banker and spoke as quietly as he had since they'd first entered the bank.

"With just a little luck, we'll be through the mountains before anyone unties you, but just in case we don't make it, Mister Blanding, here's somethin' for you think about. After that ten years in the penitentiary you talked about, you got my word I'll come back an' kill you."

Buff had finished emptying the drawers and was tying the sack closed as Henry got to his feet, eased the hammer down on his six-gun, and holstered it.

The silence was total. Buff wiped off his brow again as Henry lifted down an oaken *tranca* and eased it into the steel hanger on each side of the roadway doors. There was a large brass padlock suspended from a peg above where the door-bar had been leaning. Henry would have liked to leave the bank by the front door and padlock the place from out front, but the risk was too great.

He led Buff through the storeroom to the alley door, which had a similar oaken *tranca* barring the door from the inside. He lifted it away and eased the door open to peek out.

The alley was empty for its full length. A woman calling children to supper was the only sound. They eased out and walked quickly to the south. Dusk was on the way, which would help.

When they reached the livery barn Buff strolled in the back door, and went to look in the harness room for sign of Ed Duval. As he expected, he did not find him. This time of day Ed would be at either the cafe or the saloon.

They took the pair of horses Buff had stalled near the alley, bridled them, but left them tied until they got their own animals from across the road behind the smithy. They returned astride, turned the tandem horses loose, and gave each of them a hard cut across the rump with quirts.

The horses jumped out and lit down the alley.

Henry led off to the south, emerging from the alley onto Main Street among the shacks at the lower end of town. Buff looked back; there were two dozing horses up at Overman's tie-rack, otherwise Main Street was empty.

As they rode without haste out of town Henry reined toward a shack with four horseshoes nailed to the door. He flung the brown paper sack close to the door and reined back beside Buff.

They booted their animals into an easy, mile-eating lope and held them at it as dusk settled. Before long, dusk yielded to nightfall. They could no longer see Prairieton behind them.

Henry looked at Buff. "Hard work?"

The younger man rolled his eyes. "To tell you the truth, I don't think I'm really cut out for this. I sweated off five pounds back there."

Henry was groping for his cut plug as he replied, "If you're careful with your money, you most likely won't ever have to do it again." Then, changing the subject, "I been ponderin' about Boice. Eventually they're goin' to figure things out. Maybe not for a while, but when they do, someone'll ride down to Edgerton an' discover that us two and the bedridden feller left the country together."

Buff was turning a little more loose as they put miles behind them. He too had thought about their injured partner. "Henry, I figured out something on the drive back yesterday. Suppose we dressed Boice like an old lady and helped her board the train?"

Henry rode several yards before speaking. Then he said, "You plumb sure you aren't cut out for this? That's pretty good, Buff, if he can stand it."

"He's got to stand it, Henry. One thing, he sure as hell will look like he—she—needs help."

Henry got the cud into his cheek and leaned over to expectorate, after which he slackened to a walk, then halted. Dismounting, he tossed his reins to Buff and walked back up the road for a few yards.

When Henry returned, Buff asked, "All right?"

Henry smiled at him. "As good as I figured," he said as he remounted.

A few yards farther along Buff asked how much money Henry thought they had in the white sack tied to Henry's saddle horn.

The answer had to be a guess, but Henry had done a little hasty tallying back at the bank. "More'n I imagined. I figured we'd get four, five thousand."

Buff's eyes got perfectly round. "More'n that, for chrissake?"

"I'm guessing, Buff. Twice that an' maybe a tad more."

This time Buff did not even gasp, he rode straight up in his saddle, looking like a sleepwalker.

They picked up the gait again and held to it for a fair

distance. A loping horse could keep on loping for many miles; a running horse couldn't.

Henry did not believe there was any pressing need for fast riding. The way they had left Blanding and his clerks trussed and gagged, they would not be able to free themselves. If no one missed the banker or his clerks and came looking for them, it was likely the robbery would not be discovered until tomorrow.

But that was only part of his feeling of security. If that had been all he'd thought they could depend upon, he probably would not have robbed a bank.

The night began to turn chilly. Henry guessed they had covered more than half the distance down to Edgerton. They met no traffic until they were topping a rise and saw an early-morning stagecoach coming their way.

They veered off the road into some trees until it had passed, then returned to the road, but from there on they were watchful in both directions.

After the tension passed, they were both hungry, but nothing could be done about it until they reached Edgerton.

Henry had a question. "How will we get the right size dress for Boice?"

Buff shrugged. "Tell the store clerk it's for our aunt, and show him about how wide an' tall she is. It don't have to be a real good fit, does it?"

Henry was thinking of something else. "You got any idea when them trains run?"

"Boice knows. He made the run down here a few times with passengers who had to catch a train. He told me they run pretty often but only two of 'em stop in Edgerton, one pretty early in the mornin' an' the next one pretty late at night."

They were riding down a long-spending slope with distant rooftops in sight when Buff happened to glance back. He swore and jerked his horse off the road in the direction of a field of big rocks. Henry did the same without looking for the reason until they were fairly well hidden by huge boulders.

It was a southbound coach coming from the direction of Prairieton. If the driver had seen them, everything they had planned could be shot out of the saddle.

But the coach did not slacken pace as it whirled past with the hitch in an easy lope. As they watched the rig pass, Henry said, "I hope there's no folks aboard who lives in Prairieton."

"The driver will, sure as hell."

They went back to the road for two miles before angling away from it to parallel the road until the outskirts of Edgerton shone in new-day sunlight.

They found a bosque of black oaks and rode into it. They dismounted, and Buff held the horses while Henry pulled their shoes, tossed them into a brushy little arroyo, and took some time finding a soft place to bury the shoe pullers.

They entered Edgerton from the east. It was a fair-sized town, about twice as large as Prairieton, with quite a number of brick buildings and lots of shade trees. Near the southeast edge of town, the railroad passed through a network of loading corrals large enough to handle hundreds of head of cattle at a time.

The Edgerton Hotel, a two-story brick building, was situated on Second Street, west of Main Street, in the center of town. There were two livery barns; Henry and Buff left their animals to be cared for at the barn nearest the hotel.

They sought a cafe, put the white sack between them at the counter, and ate until even the owner, wearing a soiled apron that covered a respectable paunch, jokingly asked when they had last eaten. Henry did not look up, but Buff smiled. "Can't remember," he said. The cafeman laughed and left them.

Back outside, horseback, wagon, and buggy traffic was

already filling the roadway. Henry shook his head; he did not like towns this size, never had, and probably never would.

"Lead off," he told Buff.

Buff navigated the traffic with Henry behind him and went down to Second Street. As they passed a dry-goods store with several overblown mannequins in the window displaying the latest in lady's attire, Buff jerked his thumb.

Henry nodded and continued to walk along with the white sack over one shoulder.

CHAPTER THIRTEEN
Edgerton

WHEN HENRY AND Buff entered Boice's room he was sitting up, eating stew from a large bowl. He looked at them, put the ladle-sized spoon in the bowl, and set it aside as he said, "I was beginnin' to worry."

Henry dropped the sack beside a little table and pulled a chair around. "Nothin' to worry about," he told the large man in the bed. "We couldn't make the raid until the town was quiet, an' ridin' forty miles takes time. How are you feeling?"

"Good as new. How did it go?"

Buff sprawled on a bench as he replied, "Like clockwork."

"Blanding didn't make no trouble?"

"No. He was mad, but didn't do anything that would get him killed."

Boice jutted his chin in the direction of the white sack. "Is that the loot?"

Henry arose, picked up the sack, and before untying its mouth told Buff to lock the door. Henry upended the sack, and Boice and Brady looked on in awe as Henry began shifting the bundles of banded greenbacks into three piles. There was not a sound until he got down to the loose bills and had to count them individually before distributing them the way a poker player deals cards.

Boice said, "God a'mighty," and picked up one of the piles. "How much was there, Henry?"

99

Henry smiled a little. "That's what you got shot for, Boice. Close to five thousand for each of us."

It took a while for Buff and the man on the bed to recover. Eventually Boice said, "We ought to do this oftener."

Henry began to systematically stuff his share into pockets; he really needed his saddlebags, but they were on his rig down at the livery barn.

He sat down again, explained to Boice how they figured to get him on the train tonight, and Boice did not even frown.

Buff looked up. "All banks keep this kind of money around, Henry?"

Malden doubted it very much. "My guess is most of 'em don't keep half that much on hand. This was pure luck." He fished out his nubbin of a plug, which was all that was left, got a cheek pouched with molasses-cured, and went to the window to look out. Edgerton was a busy place. When he turned back, he said, "Buff, how about goin' back to that store and get Boice a dress an' maybe a bonnet. Some of them lace gloves ladies wear up their elbows."

Buff arose, considered his pile of new wealth, and shook his head. He could not stuff it all in his pockets as Henry had done or he'd look like a chipmunk with its cheeks full.

Henry said, "I don't know about shoes."

Boice scowled. "I don't need no women's shoes. The dress'll be long enough."

Buff cast a final glance at his wealth as he headed for the door. "Don't let nobody get near that, hear?"

After he was gone, Boice, with his share of the loot in a valley in the blankets made by his parted legs, asked Henry for the details of the raid.

It was a recitation filled with pure satisfaction. The only thing Henry thought might cause problems was that damned coach from Prairieton, but Boice replied, "What the hell. Them folks wouldn't even know the bank'd been raided that early in the morning, would they?"

That was the same thought that had occurred to Henry. He was almost confident that the trussed men at the bank could not possibly have been found before that stage left town.

Almost. The present situation had been planned to this point with considerable care. But if Henry, now in his forties, had ever learned anything from life, it was that there was some kind of natural perversity that could, and very often did, interfere unfavorably in the affairs of folks.

He went to stand by the window again. Down below, a thickly built black wagon passed along, drawn by four horses, twice as many as would normally be required on a vehicle no larger than that one was. This wagon had a heavily chained tailgate, no windows, and the word POLICE in large white letters on each side.

Henry watched the wagon until Boice got his attention by saying, "The town marshal up there's too fat an' punky to do a lot of riding."

Henry nodded and said, "Maybe. But he'll do something, for a fact. He'll have to, with the whole blessed town up in arms . . . There was a feller rode into Prairieton yesterday evening. A professional bounty hunter. Marshal Mosher said his name was Loosely. He dresses all in black."

Boice paused in fingering his mound of money to look at Henry. "Well, you laid a good trail didn't you?"

"Yep. I shod Loosely's horse. He impressed me as the kind of human buzzard who'd feel right at home in a town that's just been raided of one hell of a lot of money."

"You worryin' about him, Henry?"

Henry returned to the chair. "Not worrying, Boice, just wonderin' about him. Maybe a feller can fool a feller like the town marshal, but Loosely's an altogether different breed."

"You are worrying, Henry."

"Naw, but until we're on those steam cars tonight I'm sure goin' to keep both eyes wide open."

Buff returned, looking pleased. He put two cartons on a

table and with a flourish held up an elegant, clearly quite expensive lace dress with a maroon undergarment to go with it.

Henry sighed to himself. Nobody's feeble old aunt wore anything like that; maybe the madam of some happy house would.

Boice held up a bonnet that worked like blinders on a set of harness. Boice looked at Buff, at the things he had brought, and leaned back in bed to snort shrilly.

Henry left to get some food. It was early afternoon; Edgerton's bustle and noise was at its peak. Adding to the bedlam a train passed through, puffing great gouts of black smoke and making enough noise in the form of rattles, grinds, and snorts to awaken the dead.

Henry went first to the livery barn, got his and Buff's saddlebags, and slung them over his shoulder before returning to the same cafe where he and Buff had eaten earlier.

The place was almost empty. The proprietor with the sagging paunch looked up from reading a newspaper, remembered Henry, and sauntered down the counter, grinning. "You fellers hungry again already?"

Henry smiled back. "Well, this time you could make up some grub in three sacks."

The proprietor nodded; it was not an unusual request. "Beef an' spuds with some bread?"

"Fine," Henry agreed as he heard someone enter from the roadway. It was a spare, hawk-faced man with a badge on the front of his shirt. He and the cafeman exchanged a casual greeting as he sat down near Henry. The lawman shoved back his hat and said, "Goin' to be a hot, dry summer."

Henry nodded. "Sure startin' out that way."

"Danged cattlemen'll be drivin' in to ship as soon as the grass's gone. Earlier this year, or I miss my guess." He looked at Henry. "You ride for one of the local outfits?"

"Nope. Just passin' through. It'd be a little late to get hired on."

The lawman nodded as he reached for a pitcher of water and a glass.

The cafeman arrived with three paper sacks. Henry paid him, nodded to the lawman, and departed. The cafeman wagged his head. "That feller an' his partner was in earlier an' you never seen two fellers put away grub like they did."

The lawman's response made him laugh. "Maybe they need to be wormed."

As the cafeman brought the lawman's meal and coffee he said, "Any luck?"

"No. It's really not our job anyway. That's why the Union Pacific's got its own lawmen. They can cover more ground than we can from town. Put some riders aboard a boxcar, take 'em where the trail's fresh, an' unload 'em."

"I heard it was the Jennings brothers."

The lawman was studying his platter when he replied. "You can hear anything, Eb." He picked up his knife and fork. "I doubt it was the Jenningses—they're old hands. These fellers didn't even try to get the door open on the mail car. They went through the cars makin' folks put their money and whatnot in a sack."

"How much did they get?"

The lawman shrugged. "No tally yet, but my guess is that they got maybe two, three hundred dollars an' some stick-pins, watches, and rings."

The lawman got on with his meal and the cafeman returned to his tipped-back chair and his newspaper.

One thing the lawman had said was a fact. It was hot out, without a cloud in the sky. By the time Henry got back to Boice's room he was sweaty. He handed Boice and Buff the sacks and went to fill a glass with water before eating his own meal.

Later, Henry returned to the streets and ended up at the railroad office, where he bought passage west for himself, his brother, and his sickly aunt. The station agent, partly out of sympathy, partly out of an instinct for business, suggested a private stateroom that would be more comfortable for the ailing old lady.

Henry agreed, pocketed the tickets, and started back to the hotel. Dusk was on the way: there were long shadows on the lee side of trees and buildings. The train would stop in Edgerton at seven o'clock. The agent had said, "Sharp," then qualified that with "If it ain't delayed."

Henry stopped by the livery barn. The proprietor, a slow-moving, tired-acting man, was sitting on a bench when Henry came along. He offered Henry a cigar. Henry declined, thinking that business in a town the size of Edgerton had to be pretty good. The only thing Ed Duval up in Prairieton had ever offered him was long-winded conversation during which Ed snapped his red suspenders a few times.

The liveryman looked at Henry as he said, "You an' your partner want them horses taken up to the smithy tomorrow? I see someone already pulled their shoes. They ain't goin far barefoot."

Henry sat down on the bench. "Not tomorrow, but directly."

"Oh, you're figurin' on stayin' in town for a spell, are you?"

"For a spell," Henry replied. "Heard at the cafe it's likely to be a long, hot summer."

The liveryman trickled fragrant smoke while replying, "Sure feels that way." He considered the ash on his stogie and flicked it with a finger. "If it don't rain in time, the cowmen'll flood the place with cattle to be shipped before autumn." The liveryman plugged the cigar back between his teeth. "You a cowman, by any chance?"

Henry smiled. "Just a rider. Takes more money than I'll ever have to get into the ranchin' business."

The tired-acting man agreed. "Partner, if you don't inherit it or marry it, forget it." The liveryman had a harsh little laugh. "Go into the train-robbin' business. Two fellers stopped the eastbound out in the middle of nowhere yestiddy and went through the cars, robbin' the passengers."

"The law go after them?" Henry asked, and got a snort of disdain.

"Not Edgerton's law. We got a chief an' four policemen. One went down the tracks to the place where the train got stopped, then came back to town to say there wasn't no sign of 'em. Now what in the hell did he expect? They'd leave a sign pointin' the way they went?"

Henry sauntered down the runway to look in on his horse and Buff's animal. They were eating their heads off and did not look up.

He went on through to the alley and hiked in the direction of the hotel. He paused on the porch to scan the sky. It was getting along toward evening. This time of year it would not get really dark until about seven o'clock.

Upstairs he told Buff and Boice he had arranged for a private compartment because the station agent had thought that would be best for their old, ailing aunt.

Boice snorted.

Henry was standing at the window when a stagecoach came through with slack traces. It had come from the south, but it had PRAIRIETON–EDGERTON painted on the door.

When Henry thought it was getting close to train time, he and Buff helped Boice stand up and put on his elegant maroon undergarment, then the lace dress over it. Boice was large and thick, but the dress was still a size or two too large. He solved part of that by stuffing his loot up high under his longjohns, next to his skin.

Buff and Henry put their money in their saddlebags, Boice relinquished his shell belt and holster, but refused to part with his six-gun. He worked it down into his right-hand boot and worked the dress down to the floor so his booted feet would be covered, except when he walked.

The bonnet posed problems. It was tall enough, but Henry had to slice both seams for it to be wide enough.

Boice seemed strong enough. His injuries were healing well, and the food he'd eaten earlier had contributed to his feeling of well-being. He said he'd like some whiskey, but since there wasn't any, it was out of the question. Henry had him practice walking stooped with a slightly unsteady gait. Buff watched, seemed satisfied that in darkness Boice could pass, but grinned at the look on Boice's face. Buff said, "You got to keep your head down. In the face you don't look like no sick old woman."

Boice shot the younger man a mean look, but said nothing as he shuffled toward the door with his face forward, and shuffled back.

He looked at Henry. "Is this goin' to work?"

"Boice, sooner or later they're goin' to come searchin' down here. It won't take a real smart snooper to figure out we was here, an' since our horses will still be here, then we had to take the steam cars. Maybe two fellers with an ailin' old aunt will throw them off, at least for a spell. . . . Somethin' you both got to remember—wherever there's trains there's a telegraph. Not like up in Prairieton where any news's got to go by horseback. From here on, we're in more danger than we ever was up there."

Buff was not worried. "Henry, since you shod our horses backward, they're goin' to find tracks of two fellers riding *toward* Prairieton, not away from it." Buff paused before adding, "Them two cheeked horses'll be what they'll track north. Hell, even if they come down to Edgerton lookin' for us, it'll be a while."

Henry showed his small smile. "I hope you're right, Buff. Now let's see if we can get on that damned train."

CHAPTER FOURTEEN
A Change of Direction

IT WAS MIDMORNING before anyone noticed that neither of the steel shutters had been closed over the bank's windows and that the big brass padlock was not on the roadway door.

Will Mosher went up and beat on the door; there was no reply. He went around to the alley, pushed on the rear door, drew his handgun, and walked into the front of the building.

Jeremy Blanding's eyes blazed at him.

Mosher freed the banker first and was doing the same for his clerks when Blanding rushed to his desk, grabbed a six-gun, jammed it into the front of his britches, flung the *tranca* aside at the roadway door, and burst outside, swearing like a madman.

His clothing was soiled and awry, his face was beet red, and his usually carefully combed hair stood in all directions.

He yelled that the bank had been robbed.

People scuttled in all directions with the news. Over at the saloon Kent Overman emerged, still wearing his barman's apron. Down at the general store a number of local men appeared as Blanding yelled and waved his arms.

At the hotel a tall, dark-skinned man dressed all in black stepped to the front porch and put on his low-crowned, stiff-brimmed hat. Dougherty appeared beside him and said, "Dammit, my savings was in there."

The man beside him started walking. By the time he reached Blanding, who was gasping for breath and leaning on the brick front of his bank, Will Mosher had emerged, followed by the white-faced, unsteady clerks.

Kent called from across the road. "I heard a pair of horses running like hell out of town last night when I come out for a breath of fresh air . . . Mister Blanding, what did they take?"

"Everything! Henry Malden and that fellow who worked at the livery barn cleaned out the safe, took everything from the cash drawers." Blanding turned on the town marshal. "What'n hell you standing there for! Go after the sons of bitches!"

Mosher started south for his horse. Along the way, he was joined by Andy Collins and Kent Overman, who left his apron lying in front of the saloon as he ran to catch up.

Ed Duval, eating an early midday meal at the cafe, saw the running men and left his dinner to go outside. Everyone was yelling that the bank had been robbed. Ed stood like he'd taken root. His savings had been in the bank.

He started after the hurrying men across Main Street, but bulk and short wind kept him from arriving at his runway until the town marshal and others were leading horses out to be hastily saddled. Ed went from one to the other, except for the marshal; those were his horses they were taking. No one heeded him at all. As they burst out of the barn, Andy Collins veered toward his corralyard and yelled for someone to bring his guns.

Kent Overman tied his animal in front of the saloon, rushed inside, and reappeared in a moment, fully armed.

Townsmen emerged from the stores and houses to join the northward rush out of Prairieton behind the marshal.

Those left behind gathered like quail in little coveys to excitedly talk and gesture in the direction of the bank. Blanding and his two clerks were inside, standing like dazed creatures. For once, the banker was totally silent.

Then the rawboned man in black sauntered in and looked around before tapping Blanding on the shoulder.

"When did it happen?" he asked calmly.

"Yesterday. Right at closing time."

"You ever see 'em before?"

"See 'em before! One of them worked for the town blacksmith. The other one was the young fellow who worked for Ed Duval at the livery barn . . . Who are *you*? What's your interest?"

The weathered face looked almost pleasant as the unruffled stranger replied, "Name's John Loosely. They say anything about which way they was going?"

Blanding began to scowl. "After they left? How the hell would I know—!"

One of the clerks said, "Mister Blanding, the feller from the smithy said somethin' about goin' over the mountains. You recollect that?"

Blanding glared at his clerk before facing the man in black again. "Yeah. He did say something like that . . . Are you a lawman, Mister Loosely?"

"Not strictly speaking, Mister Blanding. You want to put a bounty on those men?"

The banker and his clerks regarded the cold-eyed man in silence as a suspicion occurred to each of them. Blanding said, "A bounty?"

"Mister Blanding, in my trade we don't hunt 'em down for exercise."

Blanding's voice softened. "I see. A bounty . . . Well, yes, two hundred dollars dead or alive—and the recovery of my money. The bank's money."

"How much did they get, in round figures?"

"Ten thousand dollars, Mister Loosely."

Again the clerk spoke up. "Closer to fifteen, Mister Blanding. Your twelve from the vault and what we had in our cash drawers."

Blanding reddened. "Mister Loosely, until we make a count I can't be sure."

The bounty hunter smiled without a shred of humor. "Two hundred dollars for each of them, Mister Blanding? They made off with something like—"

"A thousand each," Blanding blurted. "An' the return of the money."

John Loosely brushed back his coat to disclose an ivory-stocked six-gun. Down the backstrap were nine inlaid silver crosses. He waited until the three men in front had seen the gun and the little crosses, then let his coat drop forward as he said, "Gents, a thousand dollars each for 'em and the return of your money. It can't be done overnight, so be patient. But it'll be done."

Loosely got as far as the door before speaking again. "It'll help things along if not a word of our agreement gets to your town marshal."

As the tall man in black passed from sight, Blanding turned on his clerks with a snarl. "Clean the place up, and remember—that fellow was never in here and I didn't make a trade with him. Not a damned word, you understand?"

Loosely walked down to the livery barn, where Ed Duval was wringing his hands over the loss of his savings and because Will Mosher's companions would more than likely ride his horses into the ground.

When he saw the rawboned man walk in, Ed gave silent thanks they hadn't commandeered his horse, because the stranger, who dressed like a damned undertaker, did not look like the kind of man who would listen to reason. Ed already knew enough about him to hasten forward and reassure him that his animal was still there and was being well cared for.

The tall man nodded and went down the line of stalls until he found his horse. Then he leaned on the door as

Ed ranted about the damned robbery and the loss of his savings.

Loosely sauntered out back, stopped at the edge of the alley, and eased his hat back. When Duval approached, Loosely pointed to the ground. "Two horses come in here. Did you know the fellers?"

Ed scowled at the tracks. "No one come in here. When I left last night after doin' the damned chores because my dayman wasn't around, no riders had come along."

Loosely stood hip-shot. "Well now, liveryman, there is the tracks clear an' plain. Shod horses and another pair goin' north."

Ed could not refute the evidence that was in front of his eyes. If anyone had ridden in from the back alley, it must have been while he was having supper at the cafe—but there were no strange horses in his barn or among his corralled animals.

Before Ed could speak, someone entered the runway out front. Ed hiked in that direction.

It was a local cowman who wanted his horse cared for until he finished some business in town. Ed looked after the horse and was about to return to the alley when he saw the dark man strolling forward, hands in pockets, looking thoughtful. He walked past Ed as though he did not know he was standing there, returned to the roadway, and stood out there, hands in pockets, studying the town.

When Ed returned from corralling the rancher's horse, there was no sign of the stranger.

Loosely was across the road in the blacksmith shop. The banker had identified the outlaws well enough, and he'd had to listen to the fat man with the red suspenders alternately curse his dayman and shake his head over Buff's perfidy because Ed had liked his dayman.

In the blacksmith shop, where there was no one to interfere, he squatted low. The ground was like iron; it did not take imprints well but the sooty dust did: someone had pulled two sets of shoes and carelessly tossed them aside. He had then reshod the horses, but what puzzled John Loosely was that when he had led them back to their corrals, the tracks were reversed; they seemed to have been led inside instead of back outside.

Loosely returned to the rear yard and moved parallel to the tracks as he studied them again.

The explanation came to him gradually—whoever had shod those two horses had nailed the shoes on backward.

He asked a man in the roadway where the blacksmith lived, and hiked down there. The door was ajar, but he knocked anyway.

Halderman snarled at him to enter.

Inside, the house had a sour odor and very little light. The older man, who sat on a chair with his bandaged leg stretched out to another chair, looked Loosely up and down before he growled at him.

"If it's about gettin' a horse shod, I'm out of the business for a spell. Got kicked in the knee."

Loosely leaned in the doorway. "It's about your hired man."

"Henry? What about him? He's at the shop, ain't he?"

"No. Him and the liveryman's hostler raided the bank yesterday evening."

Halderman's mouth fell open. "Who the hell are you?"

"John Loosely. I need some information about Henry."

"Do you? Well now, Henry's the best man I've ever had, an' I've hired two dozen over the years . . . Robbed the bank? Where'd you hear that?"

"From the banker and his clerks."

Halderman looked at his bandaged knee for a moment, then burst into laughter. When next he spoke, he still looked amused. "You don't say. Henry robbed Blanding's damned bank?" Halderman laughed again.

"Where did Henry come from?" Loosely asked.

Halderman was quite for a moment, then put a sly look

on the weathered-dark man with the beartrap mouth and close-set eyes. "I never asked an' Henry never said. But my guess is that he come from Missouri."

"Missouri?"

"Mister, are you deef? I said Missouri, but I ain't sure. How much did they get?"

Loosely was straightening up off the doorway as he replied, "Enough." He turned and walked away.

Halderman cocked his head. When he could no longer hear footsteps he took a little brown paper sack from the side of his chair, opened it, and recounted the money it held. Eighty-two dollars.

He replaced the sack between himself and the side of the chair, watched a shiny blue-tailed fly land on his bandaged knee, and laughed again. Missouri? He'd never heard Henry mention Missouri, but it was a hell of a distance from Prairieton. Eighty-two dollars' worth away.

Will Mosher returned on a tired horse with his demoralized posse. They handed their horses over to Ed Duval, plus two others of his that they'd found six miles north of town near the foothills, bridled cheek to cheek.

Mosher went to his office, tired and sweaty, thirsty and hungry. The bounty hunter came in and asked if the posse had had any luck.

The marshal did not like to have to tell the bounty hunter that his headlong pursuit northward had netted only two horses bridled tandem to leave the impression the outlaws had escaped northward. Henry Malden and Buff Brady had been very cunning.

Loosely showed nothing on his face. He asked for as much information as the marshal had on Henry and Buff. What he got, he mostly knew, but one thing Marshal Mosher said that was interesting had to do with the stage driver fighting off bandits and getting wounded in the process, to save the bank's money. He also found out that one of the outlaws had hauled the wounded man down to Edgerton for a medical man to look over.

Loosely departed and had an early supper at the cafe before strolling up to the hotel where Dougherty was smoking a little pipe on the porch. He eyed Loosely warily as the lanky man pulled a chair around and sat down next to him. Loosely's first question was harmless. He asked if Dougherty knew how badly the stage driver had been injured. The hotelman's reply was short. "Go ask Mabel Foster, the midwife. She took care of him. All I know is that he bled a lot, but them other two fellers looked after him real well."

Dougherty knocked dottle from his pipe and pocketed it. "Hard to believe them two robbed the bank. I had a hunnert dollars in that damned bank. Been better off to have put it in a tomato can an' bury it out back."

"What happened to the stage driver?"

"That young feller, Buff, hauled him down to Edgerton in one of Ed Duval's spring wagons."

Loosely went back to the livery stable. Duval was dunging out his barn.

Ed did not allow Loosely a chance to speak. He said, "I'll never in this lousy life find another hired man as good as Buff Brady. Hell, he'd see things that needed doin' an' the next thing I knew he'd done them. He pulled the wheels on one of my spring wagons and greased the axles, even put in a new grease retainer."

Loosely nodded. "When did he do that? The day before he hauled that wounded feller down to Edgerton?"

Ed gazed steadily at the tall dark man. "The day before. Somethin' wrong with that?"

Loosely did not respond; he picked up a shank and approached the stall where his horse was dozing. Ed watched him lead the animal out and saddle it. When Loosely was mounted, Ed said, "You owe me four bits."

Loosely leaned from the saddle to hand over the money,

then evened up his reins and, to Ed's bafflement, rode down the south side of his barn to the alley. He sat his saddle for a few moments, reined southward until he had passed the last few shacks down there, then reined to the center of the road heading south.

Ed had trouble with that. He knew who the manhunter was, he knew how he made his living, and in light of what had happened last evening he thought sure as hell Loosely was on a trail, but if he was on the trail of Henry and Buff, the darned fool was riding in the wrong direction.

CHAPTER FIFTEEN

Safe . . . ?

SPRINGTIME IN THE Pawnee Valley usually arrived sullenly, often in the wake of several warm rains; they made feed grow for which stockmen were grateful, but that rainstorm a few weeks back had seen the end of those periods of warm moisture. The ground was fairly hard and dusty again.

There would be more rains, but not for a while. Springtime hung on as long as it could, then yielded to summer, an increasingly hot time of the year. Edgerton's merchants were already preparing for the hot weather even before it got there. Hotels and rooming houses had large pitchers of lemonade just inside their front doors. Lemonade to thirsty people had a dual effect; first, it quenched thirst; secondly, it blunted appetites.

It was almost dark out. East of town an incoming train let go a mournful blast from its whistle.

There was light freight to be loaded as the locomotive engine hissed and groaned. Six passengers boarded. The portly, no-nonsense individual in the vestibule relieved them of their tickets as they passed. The last three tickets he scanned, then turned with a grunt to lead the way to the private compartment. Behind him, two rangemen aided an obviously overweight and unsteady large woman.

As the conductor stood aside for them to enter, the last man handed him a silver dollar. For the first time since the train had stopped, the conductor smiled. "Anything you folks need, just pull that little cord by the window. Thank you."

It seemed like hours passed before the whistle blew, the cars jerked and clanked, and the forward momentum began to increase. Boice sat down, pushed his legs out from an upholstered seat that folded out into a bed, and watched the lights of Edgerton slide past as the train gathered speed.

Boice eased back gingerly. One of his bandages felt sticky. It was the bandage around his ribs where the bullet had gone between his ribs and the inside of his arm.

Buff stowed the saddlebags in an overhead satchel sling, made room for Boice to lie down, and asked if the large man was all right. Boice replied, "Feel fine. I got enough greenbacks under my clothes to heal just about anything a man could have."

They had been tense during their exit from the hotel and the slow walk to the train depot, right up until the conductor had closed the door. Buff loosened up a little when he lit a cigarette. Henry sat across the small distance simply gazing out the window. Neither of his companions knew it, but this was the first time Henry Malden had ever ridden a train. The almost imperceptible rocking motion coupled with the monotonous clicking sound of the wheels passing over joints in the track made him drowsy.

Boice finally sat up and got help getting the dress over his head. The rib bandage was soaked. They removed it, studied the extent of the torn scab, told Boice he would have to be careful, rebandaged the wound, and helped him get the dress down over his head and shoulders. By this point Boice needed a shot of whiskey.

Henry left the compartment, sought the conductor, and was told he had to pass through three forward cars to reach the smoking area. He bought a pony of whiskey from a burly attendant wearing a spotless white coat, returned with it to their room, and worried the cap off before handing the bottle to Boice.

The change was almost instantaneous, but after his third jolt Boice sank back and went to sleep. Buff took the bottle, considered it, decided against a drink, and handed it to Henry, who did not even glance at it as he shoved it down the side of the seat next to the window.

Henry and Buff succumbed to the rocking and clicking. The feeling that at long last they were leaving danger behind made them both relaxed.

Occasionally the train flashed past distant lights of villages or ranches as it made headway into the night. An occasional foghorn sound drifted from up front where one very large light danced upon the forward track for a fair distance ahead.

The train was carrying some freight and a mail car. There were three passenger cars behind the tender and a car that served as the dining car and smoker.

There were not a great many passengers. They could all have been put into one passenger car, except that their tickets had designated where they were to sit.

Suddenly the train lost headway, steam hissed, and brakes squealed as someone let go a fierce blast from the foghorn up front.

The jarring awakened just about everyone but Boice. Henry and Buff leaned out the windows, but it was too dark to see anything outside.

The noise stopped, the cars started easing forward again, and the conductor came along as Henry opened the stateroom door. "Goddamn free range cattle," he snarled, and marched on past.

Buff was wide awake now. He asked Henry if they would have to change trains again before they reached California.

Henry had no idea. All he knew about steam trains could have been put atop a pin without causing any crowding, but Buff did not really care. Each mile they bore westward his sense of well-being increased. He slouched, hat over his eyes, and considered for the fiftieth time since he and Henry had left those false tracks from Prairieton what he would do with all his money.

He fell asleep again without making a determination.

The dour conductor rapped on their door. Henry jerked upright, drew his six-gun, and held it in his lap as he placed his hat over it and nodded for Buff to open the door.

The conductor wanted to know if there was anything the sick old lady needed. Evidently that silver cartwheel had kindled a flow of compassion in this otherwise no-nonsense individual. Buff said the old lady was sleeping and that they had her medicine with them for when she awakened. The conductor went on his way, and Buff leaned on the door looking at Henry, who smiled at him.

Boice snored on, a hint of black stubble beginning to appear on his face. That troubled Buff but not Henry, who explained that the next town they stopped at, he would buy pants and a shirt for Boice. If asked, they would tell the conductor the old lady had got off. Boice would continue the trip feeling like what he was—a large, injured man.

Boice groaned awake and asked for the bottle. Henry gave it to him. He swallowed twice, handed the bottle back, and closed his eyes. Buff asked if he felt all right. Boice nodded without opening his eyes.

It got cold in their compartment; Henry thought it had to be past midnight. They pulled blankets from the folding beds to wrap themselves in. Henry put a blanket over Boice, who was snoring again.

Henry went in search of the conductor, who was standing in an unsteady little spot between two cars, trying to light a pipe in the wind. When Henry appeared, the conductor shoved the unlighted pipe into a pocket, looking disgusted. Henry asked above the noise when they would stop at a town. The conductor pulled out a large watch, flipped open the case, studied the spidery black hands, and snapped the watch closed as he answered.

"About an hour. We're runnin' a little late, but we'll stop at Barling Springs directly. How's the old lady doing?"

"We covered her up. She's doing as well as can be expected."

"What ails her?"

"She's got the consumption."

The conductor dwelt on that for a moment before replying. "It's a killer, no doubt about that. I've hauled a lot of them out to the south desert. It's supposed to be dry enough to help them. But mostly they're racks of bones and coughin' a lot. She's pretty hefty."

Henry was expressionless when he said, "They only figured out what she had a few months back."

"Doc Buell in Edgerton?"

"Yeah."

The conductor smiled wryly. "Was he sober when he told her?"

"Seemed sober to me."

"I've known the old reprobate twenty years. When he's sober there isn't no better doctor."

Henry nodded and turned to reach for the door back into the car when the train gave a mighty lurch; steam hissed, the foghorn blared for all it was worth, and the conductor was flung against the steel partition. He struggled upright, swearing at the top of his lungs. The train had jolted to a dead stop, the cars clanking and settling. The engine was clearly audible from where they were standing.

The conductor was still holding his watch as he looked wide-eyed at Henry. After a moment he flung open the door behind him and disappeared into the farthest passenger car.

Henry knew fear when he saw it in a man's face. He went briskly back to the compartment, where both Boice and Buff were wide awake and wondering what had caused the train to stop in the middle of nowhere.

He did not know what had stopped the train; he said it had to be something serious. Buff wondered if a car hadn't got derailed. Henry only knew that whatever had stopped the train had done so suddenly and abruptly.

For a long time the only sound was of steam being released from the boiler. Boice wrapped the blanket around his shoulders, his beard stubble more noticeable in the light of early dawn.

There was not a sound for a long time. Eventually a man's coarse laughter sounded as he said, ". . . Is that so? Well you put it in the sack anyway."

Henry and Buff exchanged a stare before Henry said, "Hide the saddlebags in one of those foldin' beds. . . . Boice, set still."

They listened, but there was no more noise for a long while until they heard spurs jangle as booted men started down the narrow corridor in front of the staterooms. An indignant passenger roared a curse, but it was cut off before he could finish it. The unmistakable sound followed of a heavy body striking a partition and falling.

Henry and Boice exchanged a look. Boice said, "I'll be double damned. Well, they don't get none of mine!"

A woman screamed in the adjoining compartment. As they heard her body strike wood as she was knocked senseless, another woman raised her voice and said, "You filthy animal."

That brought another burst of harsh laughter. Henry nodded to Boice and Buff. They both drew their six-guns and faced the door, scarcely breathing.

A second coarse voice said, "Leave her be. If you want her we'll come back when we're through. . . . Old woman, put them rings in the sack. Get the damned thing off or I'll cut your finger off an' get it!"

CHAPTER SIXTEEN
The Hand of Fate

A MAN FUMBLED roughly at their door. As he got it open, Henry and Buff fired at the same time. The bandit's cocked Colt went off as he was punched violently backward. The bullet tore through the ceiling.

The second man had a cloth sack in his left hand, a six-gun in his right hand. He had been slightly behind and to one side of the man Henry and Buff shot to death. He got off one shot with no time to aim.

Henry shot him high on the right side, and blood appeared on his filthy shirt. He flinched and thumbed the hammer back for another try. Buff fired from a raised position. The man's entire body wrenched straight up, his forehead spouting blood.

Next door a woman was screaming; otherwise, as the echoes died, there were only the engine sounds from up ahead.

Buff cocked his gun for another shot, but it was not necessary: there had been only the two men who were now sprawled in the narrow corridor, bleeding like stuck hogs.

Henry turned to one side at the sight of a slow movement. Boice had tipped forward, bleeding from the ears and nose. The second robber's solitary shot had hit Boice just above the eyes at close range. He was dead before he finished falling.

Buff still gripped his six-gun as he turned. Neither he nor Henry said a word.

Henry pushed up to his feet, wiped Boice's blood on his trouser leg, and holstered his six-gun. In the narrow corridor someone saw the dead train robbers, coughed, and retreated back the way he had come.

The smell of burnt gunpowder was almost overpowering.

Buff approached Boice, tore his dress, and pulled out handfuls of money. Henry took down one of the saddlebags and stoically pushed the still-warm bank notes in. Someone was coming; heavy footfalls sounded in a forceful, measured tread.

Henry said, "That's enough," and slung both sets of saddlebags over his shoulder, lifted his gun out, and leaned to peer into the corridor. The oncoming man was struggling to open the door leading into their car; evidently when the train had slammed to a halt it had jammed the door latch.

Henry looked over his shoulder as he hissed at Buff, "Dammit, come on. There's nothin' we can do for him."

Henry hurried down the narrow corridor in the opposite direction from the man struggling with the door. If there were people behind any of the closed stateroom doors they were being very quiet.

Henry wrenched open the door leading out of their car, and cold dawn air hit him in the face. Up ahead a man was sitting propped against a wheel of the stalled engine, which was still wheezing steam from the boilers. He did not move as Henry saw two horses tied to a metal rod and hurried toward them. He did not look at the sitting man as he addressed Buff. "Get the other one. Hurry up!"

There were lights showing from small train windows among the three passenger coaches as they rode northward, unmindful of the stranded train or the bitter cold.

They did not draw rein for a mile and might not have slackened off even then if the horses they were riding had not begun to stumble. They were poor animals that would only have been marginally better if they hadn't been abused lately.

Henry looked at his companion. Buff was fearfully watching over his shoulder. If he hadn't been so badly shaken he would have realized there could be no immediate pursuit.

Henry had both saddlebags across his lap. He held tightly to them until they dropped down to a walk, after which he methodically drew his six-gun, reloaded it as the horse plodded northward, and finally spoke to Buff in a calm voice.

"We're goin' in the wrong direction. We should be goin' east, back the way the train come. There'll be pursuit, but they won't expect us to be comin' toward it." Henry holstered the reloaded gun and turned up his collar against the cold. "We got to get better horses." They turned toward Barling Springs, the place the conductor had told him would have been the train's next stop. They would get horses there.

Buff's anxiety did not leave; they were in strange country with daylight brightening the world. As they rode, Buff continually turned his head. He was too rattled to understand that there would be no pursuit. Not for a long while anyway.

Barling Springs appeared as a scattering of buildings among a stand of pines, cottonwoods, and sycamores.

It looked to be about the size of Prairieton. The most noticeable building was the railroad station beside some loading corrals. A wide main thoroughfare ran east and west with lesser byways forking from it like the spokes of a wheel.

They stopped several hundred yards out to study the place. The sun was above the horizon, so visibility was excellent. The sun felt so good on Henry's back he took his time deciding their course of action.

There was a livery barn in the center of town with the

usual network of corrals behind it. Henry could see horses with their heads on the ground, a sure sign that someone, a dayman or a chore boy, had recently pitched feed.

Buff built and lighted his first smoke of the new day, then suggested that they ride far out and around the town to approach those corrals from the west. Henry nodded and squeezed his horse.

By the time they had completed their circle, they had watched a stagecoach leave Barling Springs, heading east. Henry wagged his head. Sure as hell the driver and passengers, if he had any, would come onto the stalled train in a couple of hours.

They rode among some goat sheds where the smell was very strong, dismounted, and scouted on foot. If someone was inside the livery barn he might amble out back while they were switching saddles and bridles to fresh horses. Buff worried less about this than Henry did; Buff knew something about liverymen and their penchant for wandering to the cafe maybe or to the saloon.

They sauntered down the alley, halted to indolently lean on the corrals gazing at the animals, watched the alley both ways, and listened to the sounds of the town.

Henry leaned close to say, "I'll look up the runway. If there's no one in there I'll wigwag with my hat. You take a couple of lead shanks from that post where they're hanging, pick out two horses, and lead 'em back where we left our critters."

Buff nodded and watched Henry heading for the opening to the barn.

Henry did not enter the barn. He stood in the doorway for a long time, then casually raised his hat, waggled it a couple of times, and reset it. He remained down there until Buff had two horses in tow and had kicked the gate closed after leading them out. He was watching Buff when a small voice startled him on his opposite side. It was a young boy, possibly eight years old, who was trying to steady a warped and discarded buggy tire with a stick. "Look out, mister, it don't go straight."

Henry moved clear and the child continued using the stick to maintain the momentum of the warped steel tire that wobbled all over the alley.

A short, wizened man wearing leather puttees entered from up front, saw Henry in back, and walked with a bow-legged gait toward him as he called ahead.

"Somethin' I can do for you, stranger?"

Henry had enough time to appraise the elfin-looking man and organize his reply. He smiled as he said, "Just stepped up here to avoid a kid rolling a buggy tire."

The old man leaned, looked northward where the child was valiantly making erratic progress with his warped circlet of steel, and nodded. "That's the town marshal's lad. He's supposed to be at the schoolhouse." The man turned with a rheumy look in his smiling eyes. "Bert'll take a switch to him. We got a new schoolmarm—she don't send notes, she goes directly to the house of kids skippin' school."

Henry nodded and walked away. The liveryman stood a moment watching him, then made his way back up the runway.

Buff had already saddled the fresh animals and was nervously holding the two sets of reins when Henry appeared. As they were riding west Henry recounted his adventure with the child and the liveryman. Buff listened with little interest. There was a fair amount of traffic around Barling Springs; several horsemen loping toward town from the west waved in the distance. Buff and Henry waved back and eventually turned southward to go around town in that direction.

Buff was not convinced heading back in the direction they had fled at dawn was a good idea, but Henry simply kept riding and Buff followed him.

Once they saw a solitary rider in the distance, heading

for Barling Springs. If he saw them he gave no indication of it. Later, along toward midafternoon, they had an even more distant sighting, this time of what could have been four or five horsemen. They too were heading toward Barling Springs, and that bunch held Henry's attention until they were no longer visible.

They halted at a little warm-water creek to tank up and rest the horses, both big, strong animals in their prime. Neither of them was branded.

Henry had his diminishing plug of molasses-cured to take the edge off his hunger, but all Buff had was his sack of smoking tobacco and its accompanying wheat straw papers. They rode almost all day.

Buff killed his smoke atop the saddlehorn and studied the countryside. The land was improving, there were fewer rocky places and an occasional tree. By the time dusk was deepening toward nightfall there was buffalo grass in stirrup-high clumps, healthy pines and oaks, and cattle. Not many at first, but the farther they rode the more cattle they saw. After nightfall they heard them.

Without bedrolls, they sought a protected place, gathered deadfall twigs, and built a little fire. Dead wood did not smoke, but any kind of light could be seen a long way in the night. Their fire was behind some tall gray rocks that looked like they'd been squatting there since time began.

With the horses hobbled to graze, warmth from the fire keeping the night chill at bay, they got some rest.

Buff fell asleep against his rock. Henry looked at him and remembered that Buff had told him he wasn't sure he was cut out to be an outlaw. Well, he sure was one now. Not only had they robbed the bank in Prairieton, now they were riding stolen horses. In some places a horsethief was lynched quicker and hung higher than a bank robber.

CHAPTER SEVENTEEN

A Tireless Rider

WHEN THE HORSE trader in Barling Springs discovered that two of his best saddle animals had been stolen, he said, "For chrissake, in broad daylight!"

The rawboned man in soiled and dusty black britches and coat drew on a cigar, eyeing the old man. "You didn't see 'em?"

The old man turned on John Loosely. "See 'em! You think I'd have let 'em ride off on my horses if I'd seen 'em! Only thing I seen all afternoon was a kid rolling an old buggy tire up the alley, an' a feller out there who had to get out of the kid's way."

"What did he look like?"

"Like any other damned cowboy you ever seen."

"Was he alone?"

"I just told you, all I seen was him an' that kid."

"Medium-sized young feller, was he? Maybe carrying a pair of saddlebags?"

"He wasn't young, maybe forty, average-lookin', needed a shave and a shearing. Sort of quiet, calm feller."

"Those two worn-down horses someone found in their garden patch and brought to you . . ."

"Yes, I'd guess they was ridin' them. I got 'em in the public corral out back if you want to look at them."

Loosely sat comfortably pulling on his cigar. "I already looked at them." He tipped ash onto the harness-room floor. "They belonged to those two fellers that got killed tryin' to rob the train west of here."

The older man looked puzzled. "Then who rode them?"

"Two other fellers. The same ones that killed the train robbers. Henry Malden and Buff Brady. They had a partner, but he got killed durin' the gunfight on the train. His name was Candless."

"Outlaws, was they?"

Loosely nodded. "Raided the bank up in Prairieton." As he arose to brush ash off his front he smiled bleakly at the liveryman. "They went east from here."

"How do you know that?"

"Because before dark I picked up the tracks of two fresh-shod horses goin' down your back alley south, until they turned east. Nice talkin' to you, friend."

Loosely strolled to his saddled horse out front and rode out of town.

The bounty hunter did not stop for the night. He shrugged into a sheepskin-lined leather coat that reached to his knees, buttoned it to the gullet, and let his big horse take its time. The moon was less than full, but once he was clear of Barling Springs he had little difficulty sighting the only pair of fresh-shod horse tracks going east.

There was always the possibility that he might be following the wrong sign, but in this instance he did not think so. Before leaving Edgerton he had watched an irate local lawman lead a posse heading for the stalled train. Lawmen like that did not exactly amuse him, but he'd smiled anyway; they characteristically followed hunches, which meant that after finding the train, they too would ride for Barling Springs, would arrive there in time for supper, and bed down.

It was, he had often told himself, the difference between men who got a monthly wage and those who were self-employed. Self-employed folks had to work harder, longer hours and miss an occasional meal, but in the end they made more than wages.

He lit a fresh cigar, shielding the flame inside his hat, watched the stars, and stopped occasionally to be certain he was on the right trail.

After dawn broke, it took a while for the morning to warm up. The sky was overcast, the kind of clouds that usually meant rain was on the way.

Tracking without too much sunlight was easy, particularly when there were only two sets of tracks to follow.

Near noon Loosely halted at a warm-water creek to water his horse and to study the country ahead; he saw some trees, tall grass already going to seed, and occasional jumbles of rocks. The manhunter rode wide around them out of habit. He did not expect to be bushwhacked, but he was always cautious.

He found a pile of coals behind a large rock, and cropped grass where two horses had spent the night.

His estimate was that by riding all night he had closed the distance considerably. His prey seemed unwilling to ride fast, and that too helped. It also preserved the strength of those two stolen horses in the event it might be needed later, but Loosely did not believe this manhunt would end in a horse race. But if it did, that was why he'd spent four hundred dollars for the horse he rode, about four times the going price for riding stock in cow country.

By afternoon the sun was shining. Loosely had tracked his prey in the direction of Leesville, a town on the far side of the Missouri River.

Leesville was too distant for railroad surveyors to have considered it as a depot or shipping point, and it was not as large or bustling as Edgerton. But it had one attribute: it was not very far from the Colorado–New Mexico line. Then southward was Mexico, about the only safe haven for fugitives from north of the border. It was only marginally safe, however. Although neither U.S. lawmen nor soldiers were allowed down there in pursuit, renegades who made it ahead of possemen were more likely to get shot off their horses for the boots they wore and the horses they rode than was ever the case north of the border.

John Loosely had, in fact, waylaid outlaws trying to get over the line, but he was convinced the men he was trailing had no intention of making for the border. If that had been their intention they would have begun the long ride southward before this.

Buff saw the rooftops first and yelled to Henry, who was as surprised as his partner was to find a town. There were no telegraph poles apparent, and the tree-lined roadways looked inviting. Buff thought sure as hell there'd be a saloon and a cafe, maybe even a hotel with a bathhouse out back.

In fact, as they crossed the stage road a mile or so above town, Buff saw no reason for them to avoid the place. They'd covered a hell of a lot of ground since Barling Springs, and even more from Edgerton and Prairieton. Buff had in mind a little socializing at a saloon, maybe even some hot food and a real bath.

Henry did not deny the blandishments of the town, but he just kept right on riding across the stage road and beyond. He did not argue nor remonstrate. Later, however, with shadows forming, they encountered a stand of trees on the far side of Leesville. Henry rode in, dismounted, and as he tugged loose his latigo he said, "Buff, we're well south an' east of where I figure they'll be lookin' for us, specially since by now they figure we rode west from Barling Springs, but all the same, the fewer folks who see us, the better."

Buff reddened. "Henry, for chrissake, we got to stop somewhere."

"All right, but stay out of the saloon. Just get us some food and come back."

Buff turned with a smoky gaze. They'd been partners for a long time now; yet Henry at times talked down to him like he was a little kid. It had never set well and it did not set well now. But Buff was fond of the older man, so he chose his words carefully.

"I'll ride in, get our supplies, and ride back. But it wouldn't hurt to have a pony of whiskey, too, would it?"

Henry did not answer the question. "Be real careful, Buff."

The younger man reined out of the trees. He was not angry so much as resentful. Eventually, when they could quit running, he was going to take his split of the money and put a lot of things behind him as he rode off, including Henry Malden. It was possible to like someone like Henry and still not want to be around him too long.

It felt good to be heading toward town lights as dusk settled, to be free to do his own thinking for a change.

Henry got comfortable among the trees, listened to the hobbled horse cropping grass—a very pleasant, relaxing sound to any horseman—and studied the sky through the stiff tops of the pines. It looked like rain and it felt like it, but most of all the air had that faint brimstone scent to it that meant rain sure as hell.

Henry liked that prospect. He did not have to be a seasoned outlaw to realize that horses left tracks; there was no way to get around it.

If anyone among the posse riders from Edgerton or Barling Springs was reasonably shrewd at reading sign, he would probably be back yonder somewhere. If it had rained yesterday or even today, it would have washed out their tracks, but it hadn't rained.

It would shortly, either tonight or tomorrow. Maybe someone might trail them as far as Leesville, but when it rained that would be as far as they could go.

He was tired. When a man passed forty he refused to believe that tiredness did not come from too many hours in the saddle, but it did. He felt no urge to sleep, although he hadn't had a decent sleep in a long while. He hadn't slept well back among those big rocks where they'd camped last. Every damned sound back there had snapped him wide awake.

The moon shone a sickly pale glow above the dark, lowering clouds. He spat out his cud, arose to look at the horses, sprayed amber, and walked restlessly among the trees. Their camp was less than a mile from town. Buying tobacco, some food, and a pony of whiskey shouldn't have taken this long.

Well, somewhere down all the tomorrows Henry and Buff would ride in different directions. Until that day they were partners. Henry knew there were things about Buff he was not fond of—something that used to annoy Henry, and Boice too, was the way the darned fool would practice with his six-gun when they were out hunting cattle. Without warning Buff would draw and fire at something, a rock or a flying bird or a harmless gopher snake. Invariably this caused their horses to throw a fit. He had never got Henry or Boice bucked off, but one time Boice almost ended up in some rocks and got mad. . . .

Without any warning gunshots erupted among the lighted buildings in Leesville. Henry's breath stopped for a moment and his stomach knotted.

Henry swiftly bridled and saddled his horse, and was riding out the far side of the spit of trees within minutes. The two saddlebags were in his lap, as he had carried them before. About a hundred feet west of the trees the first raindrops fell. It was open country for a fair distance. He could see only a short distance ahead, but his concentration was not ahead, it was back the way he had come.

Whatever had happened in that town, the chances were slight that Buff had survived gunfire, but if he had, and could get on horseback, he would come in a belly-down run. Henry rode out at a walk, although anxiety made it hard for him to keep the horse's gait slow.

The rain did not start to pelt him hard until he could dimly make out some trees ahead. South of the trees was a steady, square glow, the kind made by a coal oil lamp close to a window.

He could not make out the buildings very well; they seemed clustered around a yard, but with the increasing storm he soon could no longer see even the light.

Getting drenched did not create problems for a long while. He halted occasionally, listening for a horse far back. If there was one, or even more than one, he could not hear them over the racket made by the downpour.

He got in among some huge old pines, shrugged into his jacket, and was more wet inside than outside. As he resumed riding a tongue of blue-white lightning arced with a sound of snapping electrical current, then blinded both Henry and his horse as it struck in the near distance and set a pine tree afire. It burned like a very tall candle, the rainfall not inhibiting the flames at all.

The horse stumbled, quivering all over. Henry used both knees to keep him going.

The rain came in sheets, like advancing walls of water. Henry lowered his head for water to run off the front of his hat.

Henry rode stoically. He had been caught out like this before, but the other times he'd had a yellow slicker tied behind the saddle.

Instinct was all he had to tell him which way he was going, but this had happened before too. Henry had the outdoorsman's feel for directions. He may have yawed a little one way or another, but his main route was still east.

There was more lightning, but farther off. Each time, the horse humped up a little but made no problems, which was just as well; it was one thing to stay atop a pitching horse on a dry saddle and something altogether different to do it on a wet one.

The downpour became slightly erratic as a blustery wind

arose. Henry heard a dog bark once; he did not doubt there were ranches around, although he did not see any buildings for about three hours. Then all he saw was a rough old log house with a sagging ridgepole. He guessed it was not inhabited, but did not ride close to find out.

He had just one abiding thought, which was to keep riding, put as much distance as he could between himself and that town back yonder, to be far ahead when the rain stopped. Too far ahead, he thought, to be found by accident; he surely would not be tracked, not after this wild rainstorm had struck.

He rode hunched, head down, listening to storm sounds but thinking of something else: Buff Brady.

He knew as well as he knew his name some of those gunshots had been made by Buff. He also knew that if Buff got out of Leesville alive it would be a miracle. He felt a little guilty too for not having insisted that Buff stay among the trees with him.

When the rainfall became little more than a drizzle, Henry figured he had covered maybe fifteen miles. Once the water stopped coming down, the mud underfoot would take every step his horse made and mold it into tracks a blind man could follow.

He had to make some kind of a change or stand an excellent chance of being ridden down, tracks or no tracks. If he went north he could find the railroad tracks again, but that could be a serious mistake if the train passed through Edgerton on its way west, which it surely would do.

When the downpour finally stopped, even the drizzle tapering down to a gray mist, sunrise was close. Visibility was better, but not a whole lot, and he was no longer where there was timber, only rolling grassland as far as he could see.

He came upon a band of cattle who drifted, backs humped against the storm, heads down. They had been branded recently; the scabs were still in place.

CHAPTER EIGHTEEN
A Big Horse

HE SAW THE leaning wagon from a considerable distance. In open country with a new sun and spanking-clean air, a man could almost see tomorrow.

But for the big horse between the shafts Henry might have thought the wagon had been abandoned with a broken wheel. Driving anywhere after the kind of storm that had cowed the countryside last night, would sure as hell make heavy mud balls between wagon spokes.

The rig was about the size and build of a peddler's wagon, but it had a new-looking waterproof canvas top stretched across the bows.

Henry began reining slightly northward to go far around the wagon. Someone would come back for the horse.

He twisted to look in all directions. There was not a building in sight, just a few cattle and that rig leaning badly on one side.

His horse walked with his head turned in the direction of the wagon; except for that, Henry probably would not have seen the man climb down out of the wagon and raise a hand to shield his eyes as he stared at the approaching rider. One moment later the man began to shout and gesture wildly. Henry did not stop, but as he came parallel with the wagon, well to the north, the man's agitation increased. He yelled indistinguishable words and beckoned with both arms.

Henry kept on riding.

The man stumbled through hock-deep mud in a frantic run to overtake Henry. Henry drew to a halt with both hands atop the saddlehorn, watching the man. A busted wheel, even with the nearest town over fifteen miles west, was not the end of the world. All he had to do was take that big horse off the wagon and ride him bareback to Leesville or maybe some nearby ranch.

Henry could now hear the man's pleading words, not all of them but enough; the man was standing in mud halfway to his knees and he looked and sounded like someone irrational from desperation.

Henry turned back toward the wagon. The man watched until he was sure which way the horseman was going, then turned to flounder back to the tailgate of the wagon.

Henry had thought he was a young man, but he wasn't. In fact, when he got close enough for the man to start begging for help in a quavering voice, Henry thought he might be even older than Henry.

He had once been attired in matching coat and trousers of a sombre dark blue; his hat was cloud gray and good quality. What impressed soggy Henry the most was that except for mud almost to his knees, the stranger showed no sign of having gotten soaked last night. Whoever had waterproofed his wagon canvas had evidently done a very good job.

The man was babbling something about his wife, a baby, and a broken axle.

Henry peered inside the wagon. A large woman swaddled in blankets groaned and rubbed her huge belly.

Henry climbed over the tailgate. The woman's eyes were dilated and glassy as she grabbed Henry's hand and squeezed with surprising force. She was perspiring and her lips were dry.

She looked enormously distended. Henry lifted some of the blankets and put them down slowly. He looked at the man, who was gouging wood on the tailgate with his fingernails. He had been ashen before; now he was white to the hairline.

Henry positioned himself so that the man's view was obstructed by Henry's back. He drew the blankets back carefully. Some of them were soaked. He rocked back on his heels and felt like swearing. He'd seen the water sacks break on a hundred cows.

The husband exclaimed, "She needs a doctor."

The man was beginning to get on Henry's nerves. He turned with a growl. "What doctor, for chrissake? What were you doin', haulin' her around in her shape in that damned storm?"

"Trying to get her to the midwife in Leesville. The storm didn't hit until we was a few miles north. . . . Help her, for god's sake!"

Henry leaned forward, rolled up his soggy sleeves, and ignored the agitated man behind him.

The woman arched her back and groaned through locked jaws. Henry felt water under his soggy shirt. It was sweat. He waited until she arched again before pushing one of the blankets under her. She groped for his hand. He returned her forceful squeeze as he quietly said, "You're doin' fine. Just sink back down for a moment, then try again." Oddly, the nearly unconscious woman obeyed. Henry watched for a moment, then leaned over to do as he'd done with a hundred hung-up calves. He got a hand beneath the emerging wet tiny body and steadied it as he said, "Once more, lady. Harder this time."

But the infant scarcely moved despite her straining. Henry ran a hand across his sweaty forehead, waited, then repeated, "Once more, harder."

The woman tried but was too weak. Henry leaned with both hands this time, and as the woman strained feebly, he did too, gently and slowly. Periodically he would stop so the woman could lie and pant for a while.

The last time he exerted more pressure than the woman did. The tiny, slippery baby slid out into his hands. He said, "Lie back now an' breathe deep."

In an unsteady, hoarse voice she said, "Is she all right?"

Henry's back ached as he dried the baby on a blanket. He looked at the baby's stomach. Cows bit the cord to break it, if it had not broken during the birthing. He reached in his pocket for his small knife. In a slightly stronger voice the woman repeated the question "Is she all right?"

Henry nodded. "Lively little cuss. Doin' fine, ma'am."

"Oh thank God. Lilly. We named her months ago. Where is my husband?"

Henry was slow answering. "Outside. But lady, your lily has a stem."

For a second the woman was silent. "It's not a girl?"

"No ma'am, it's a husky little boy."

"Can you please put him up here where I can hold him?"

Henry cut the cord, and tied the end in a tight knot. The child did not even wince. He leaned to place the baby beside the mother.

He clenched his teeth and sat back, watching the sweating woman with the dank dark hair and the exhausted angelic expression tuck the baby close.

Out front the big horse between the shafts moved, and the wagon listed even more. Henry pushed two satchels against the mother to prevent her from sliding, and started to straighten up. He turned, moved on all fours to the tailgate, and looked out where steaming ground under a bright yellow sun showed an empty land.

His horse was gone!

He climbed out, leaned against the tailgate, and saw two saddlebags lying in mud where they had slipped from the saddle as the frantic man had sprung atop Henry's horse and started furiously toward Leesville. The tracks were as plain as day.

His carbine was with the saddle. As he turned to look inside, the woman began to cry as she held her tiny bundle close. It was warm inside the wagon. In another couple of hours it would be downright hot in there.

Henry hitched up his shell belt and pushed through mud to the front of the rig, where the big horse turned to watch him. It had tried a couple of times to pull the wagon, and although he was a large animal, about sixteen hundred pounds, he could do no more than gouge the broken axle deeper into the ground.

Henry turned again to scan the countryside. There was nothing moving in any direction. The father of the baby in the rig could not have been gone more than an hour, not long enough to reach Leesville in mud, but he would eventually get there.

Henry studied the big horse. It did not look like a combination horse, one that had been broken to ride as well as pull. Combination horses were not exactly rare, but few stockmen, and no horsemen, broke sixteen-hundred-pound horses to ride, because they were just too outsized and unhandy to be used under saddle.

Henry hesitated for a moment, then went to work taking the big horse from between the shafts. If that damned rattlebrained husband had ridden to Leesville, he would certainly return with help, and Henry could not risk that. He and the big horse eyed each other. The big horse would be better than walking.

He returned to the area of the tailgate, picked up the pair of saddlebags, skivved mud off them, and left them on the tailgate as he went forward to lead the horse back there.

He maneuvered the big horse as close as he could to the tailgate, then climbed up so that when he jumped he'd land astraddle the big horse.

His final preparation involved placing both saddlebags, one behind the other, about where a saddle would have gone. If he rode the horse out the saddlebags would stay with him; if the horse pitched him off, which he did not expect to happen, the saddlebags would go off with him.

From inside the wagon the woman said, "What are you doing?"

He turned to face her, crouching. "You'll be fine. Your husband stole my horse. He most likely headed for a town west of here some miles. I can't wait for him to get back. First chance I get I'll turn your harness horse loose but right now I need him."

"You could wait until my husband returns," the woman said.

"That's exactly what I can't do, ma'am."

Her eyes widened slightly as the small bundle at her side squirmed but otherwise seemed disinclined to move much or make noise. She addressed Henry again, in a quieter, softer tone of voice. "You can't just ride off. You delivered my baby. We owe you more than I can say. What is your name?"

Henry's back was bothering him again from leaning forward to see inside the wagon. "You just lie still until your husband gets back. It's goin' to get hot inside the rig, but you got a canteen an' maybe the heat will be good for the baby."

". . . Please, what is your name?"

Henry turned, straightened up, eyed the saddlebags, took one rein in his hand, and jumped.

He came down atop the saddlebags. The big horse bunched but did not move, too surprised and startled to do anything but stand rigidly still.

Henry talked to him. Both his ears were turned back. He seemed either unwilling or afraid to move with the man on his back. One thing was immediately clear to Henry:

the big horse not only wasn't a combination animal, but may never have had anyone on his back before.

Henry knew better than to use knee pressure to get the horse untracked. He pulled a little on the left rein, let slack lie for a moment, then pulled again. This time the big horse obeyed the pressure and started around to the left.

He took several steps. Henry eased back to stop him, then gently applied pressure to the right. The big horse did not hesitate this time, he moved massively and heavily, obeying the rein.

Henry smiled for the first time in two days. He lined the horse out pointing east, and when the horse stopped, perhaps waiting for another tug to the left or right, Henry applied a little knee pressure.

Henry had two seconds to discover that this horse *had* been ridden before. He ducked his head before Henry could prevent it with the reins, bawled like an enraged bull, and bucked. Not hard at first and in a straight line, but only the first few jumps. With astonishing speed for so large an animal, he swapped ends and gave Henry a moment to realize that not only had men tried to ride this horse before, but that during the course of those encounters, the big harness horse had perfected a bucking horse's techniques of sunfishing. The horse went straight up and down in a jump that could snap half the bones in a rider's body, then jammed his head between his front feet and bucked from side to side.

Henry and the saddlebags went off in a birdlike soar to land in soft mud. He was slow arising. The big horse was standing a few feet away, looking back at him.

Henry picked up the saddlebags and wiped the mud off them.

The big horse allowed Henry to walk up, pull the reins over his head, and lead him over to be tied to the left side of the wagon. He silently squeezed off as much mud as he could, used a bandana to wipe his face, walked over to the tailgate, and looked in. The woman looked steadily back. "That horse can't be ridden."

Henry leaned on the tailgate. "You didn't want to tell me that before?"

"I wasn't sure you were going to try, Mister . . . ?"

Henry hitched around to sit on the tailgate. Oddly enough his back was not causing pain. He kicked his muddy boots back and forth, gazing westward. The sun was climbing, and by now the woman's husband would be close to Leesville. She spoke to his back. "I think I can help you."

He replied without turning. "All you had to do was say that damned horse couldn't be rode."

"If you'd only wanted to ride away I don't think you'd have bothered with two sets of saddlebags."

Henry turned to gaze at the woman. "It won't matter, lady, I can't run in the mud and I can't ride that big horse. I'm goin' to be settin' here when your man and some others get back."

She ignored that. "Bring the saddlebags in here. I'll put them under me among the blankets."

He gazed at her for a long time without saying a word, then he wagged his head, turned fully, and crawled inside with the saddlebags. When she tried to raise up he told her not to strain, and worked the saddlebags beneath her inside the blankets.

She said, "They won't search me."

"Who won't, ma'am?"

"Whoever is after you and those saddlebags."

Henry used a damp, soiled sleeve to push drying mud off his forehead. "Who are you?" he asked, and got a reply he might have expected. "I know who I am. I don't know who you are."

"Name's Smith, ma'am." Henry made a crooked little smile.

She smiled back. The baby made a gasping wail, she

nodded toward the tailgate without saying a word, and Henry crawled back out into the steamy world of dazzling sunshine and high humidity.

As Henry waited with his back against the tailgate, he recalled a common saying among men. "The things a man don't need are a biting dog, a kicking mule, and a smart female." Right now he would still agree with the first two, but he had doubts about the last.

CHAPTER NINETEEN

Leesville

AS HE WAITED in wagon shade, Henry thought about how even the best of plans could deteriorate into situations where a man had to improvise. After all the clever schemes and fancy ideas about how to steal money without getting caught, here he was, helpless, waiting for the inevitable retribution.

The sun was well off center when Henry finally saw them coming, not in any hurry. It looked like a small army. He chewed, spat, and called to the woman that help for her was on the way. She did not answer.

He counted five of them. Only when they were close did he see the steel axle one was carrying and the tools two of the others had along.

He recognized the foremost rider: it was the woman's husband riding a different horse. Beside him, with a badge on his jacket front, was a lean, hawk-faced, darkly tanned man with gray at the temples. These two did not take their eyes off Henry.

Henry neither spoke nor moved until the lawman gestured with a gloved hand. "Drop the gun, mister."

Henry dropped it in the hardening mud before they all swung off their mounts. Three of them went to study the wagon from above and beneath, then silently went to work with a large ratchet jack.

The woman's husband crawled inside the wagon and attended to his family.

The lawman asked Henry, "What's your name?"

Henry answered without a qualm. "Smith. What's yours?"

The lawman's eyes narrowed. "Mendenhall. Sheriff Mendenhall. We got your partner on ice back in Leesville, Mr. Malden."

Henry's lips flattened slightly, but he remained silent.

Mendenhall said, "that was foolish, sendin' him to town like that. Mister Loosely recognized his horse as one stolen in Barling Springs."

Henry's eyes did not leave the sheriff's face. "So you shot him," he murmured.

The lawman's gaze momentarily wavered. "No, Mister Loosely shot him. He had been trailing you fellers from up at Edgerton. He was to collect a bounty on the pair of you from a banker up in Prairieton. On top of that you stole two horses at Barling Springs, which he told me about, and—"

"What happened?" Henry asked coldly.

Sheriff Mendenhall's gaze wavered again. "All I know is what I was told."

"Spit it out, you son of a bitch!"

Mendenhall reddened, his right hand fell to the handle of his gun. His temper was rising when Henry spoke again, with both arms crossed over his chest. "Draw it! Go ahead!"

The three men a short distance away were motionless and staring. The sheriff had a throbbing vein in the side of his neck. He pointed to the horse the man inside the wagon had ridden. "Get up there," he snarled. "Make a quick move an' I'll kill you. *Get on!*"

Henry eyed the dozing horse, approached it from the left side, felt the cinch, which was snug enough, and mounted.

The sheriff and Henry headed for Leesville while the others worked on the axle.

The muddy men beside the wagon watched the sheriff

and his prisoner ride off. One of them, younger than the other two, said quietly, "Jeff, how much you want to bet that man don't make it to town alive?"

The burly man turned. "The sheriff would love nothing better'n to shoot that outlaw in the back for tryin' to escape. Anyone who's been around Leesville as long as I have knows Mendenhall has a quick temper and a fast gun."

A thin man with one hand on the wagon-jack, smiled at Jeff and the youth. "We goin' to get that busted axle out from under there or goin' to stand around?"

The burly man continued to watch the two riders heading west. He eventually shook his head and went back to work.

The humidity was higher as the day waned. The walking horses sweated and their riders did too. Not a word was said between the lawman and his prisoner, but after a few miles, Henry addressed the sheriff. "Loosely recognized the horse Buff was riding, then what?"

This time Mendenhall seemed to relish what he said. "He shot the kid."

"Sheriff, I was close enough to town to hear that gunfight. There was more than one shot."

Mendenhall said, "Loosely pulled his gun and gave the kid a chance to give up, but your pardner drew on him. Loosely winged him. It knocked the kid down but he wasn't dead. The kid got off two rounds real fast. One slug hit the doorjamb, the second one was a tad lower, it creased Loosely over the left shoulder. Loosely walked toward the kid firing."

Henry hung his head in silence.

It was late when they reached Leesville. After leaving their horses with the nightman at the livery barn, the sheriff gave Henry a rough shove and said, "North up the sidewalk."

The jailhouse was dark and clammy when they entered.

Mendenhall pointed to a far wall. "Go stand over there, an' if you want to try something before I get the lamp lit, go right ahead."

Henry stood with his back to the wall until the office was alight. Mendenhall kicked open a wooden door with steel reinforcements on both sides of it and herded Henry into a sour-smelling cell. After he locked Henry in, he said, "Circuit-ridin' judge is due here any day. Where is that money you stole from the bank up in Prairieton?"

Henry turned his back as he said, "Go to hell."

Mendenhall, who was easily angered, gripped the bars. "I'll bring Loosely down here in the morning. Between the two of us we'll help you remember where that money is."

Henry turned. "If Loosely knows where it is, that'll be the last you'll see of him or the money."

"We'll see about that, horsethief."

Sheriff Mendenhall went back to his office, slammed the cell door, and locked it from the office side.

With that door closed, what little light had been in the cell was blocked out. Henry felt his way to a wall bunk and sat down.

He thought about several things. The saddlebags with the woman in the wagon was not one of them.

He blamed himself for letting Buff ride into Leesville alone.

He lay back in darkness, listening to the dwindling sounds of Leesville. With no way to know what time it was he had to guess it was very late and closed his eyes.

Sleep came when he had not thought it would. He did not stir until the sun was climbing and someone warping steel over an anvil awakened him. He lay there listening; it was a good sound. He was still lying there listening when someone rattled the heavy reinforced door up front.

Expecting to see Loosely and the sheriff together, he looked out and saw only Mendenhall. He stood up slowly. The sheriff shoved a tray of food toward his prisoner and said, "The circuit rider's in town." Then, in a slightly different tone, he added a little more. "That was him in the busted wagon, for chrissake. When he come chargin' into town all he yelled about was his wife dyin' in childbirth out yonder. On the ride back out there he wouldn't talk of nothin' else. Mister Malden, this is the last day you'll see sunlight for a hell of a long time. They got Loosely patched up enough to testify. When he gets through you'll be lucky if you breathe free air again until you're old and toothless."

Henry waited out Mendenhall's outburst then mildly said, "I told you, my name is Smith."

The sheriff stood a moment looking triumphantly into the cell. He smiled. "Loosely'll be along directly. We'll have maybe an hour to beat out of you where you cached that money." Then he walked back up front and slammed the heavy door.

Henry went to the rear of the cell where sunlight was coming through a narrow steel-barred window, too high for him to see out of even if he'd had something to stand on.

Leesville was bustling. He could hear wheeled vehicles passing in the roadway, men calling back and forth. Henry returned to the bunk and perched on the edge of it, and now he thought of the money.

The woman in the wagon had not said who her husband was and Henry had not asked. He had assumed he was a cowman, maybe a cattle buyer; actually he had not thought much about the man at all after he discovered the man had stolen his horse.

One thought struck him like a blow. The judge's wife had all the evidence in the pair of saddlebags the law would need to put him in the penitentiary or hang him.

Mendenhall sat in his office. He was impatient. He had enough charges to get his prisoner put on trial, but he had no actual evidence. Everything depended on the word of the damned bounty hunter. Unless they could get the prisoner to talk. . . .

Sheriff Mendenhall went to stand in the jailhouse doorway looking across the road and up and down it. He even went down to the rooming house to look for Loosely.

CHAPTER TWENTY
The Law

HENRY DID NOT touch his breakfast until nearly noon, then all he consumed was cold black coffee. He had no appetite.

The sheriff came down and unlocked the cell door. He was red in the face. When he jerked his head for Henry to precede him up the dingy corridor he said, "Damned judge wants to have the hearing right now."

John Loosely was sitting in a chair when Henry entered the office. The bounty hunter and the sheriff exchanged a look Henry could not decipher.

Mendenhall handed Loosely a sheet of paper and said, "Read it. Be ready to answer these questions for His Honor. I don't know this judge—usually the circuit-rider is an old gaffer named Driffel. Don't let him tangle you up with questions."

Loosely tossed the paper back atop Mendenhall's desk. "I told you all that stuff. I'll remember." Loosely's eyes slid to Henry. He stared without saying a word. Sheriff Mendenhall reread the paper he'd given the bounty hunter to read, leaned back when he had finished, and also looked at Henry. "You just might get hung. Killin' those two fellers on the train—"

Henry snorted.

Mendenhall's eyes narrowed, his face reddened. "If the damned court don't settle with you, Malden, I will. You can believe that!"

Loosely shifted in the chair; apparently his wounded

151

shoulder bothered him. He fished out a stogie and lit it without taking his eyes off Henry. When he had a head of smoke rising he said, "Malden, there might be a way out."

Henry had no trouble with the implication. He remained expressionless as he return the other man's gaze.

Sheriff Mendenhall abruptly arose and walked quickly to the roadway door, opened it, and closed it after himself. When they were alone Loosely said, "That's better. Now we talk straight out. Where is the money from the Prairieton raid?"

Henry stood silent, giving the bounty hunter look for look.

Loosely removed the stogie, tipped off ash, and did not plug the cigar back between his teeth. "I'll tell you something you'd maybe like to know. You're not goin' to leave this town alive."

Loosely waited for the significance of that to sink in before speaking again. "Sheriff Mendenhall hates your guts."

Henry finally spoke. "But you could save my bacon?"

"Well, in a manner of speaking. I got wounded at the saloon. Hold it—let me finish. What happened up there is over and done with. I got Brady's gun and everything from his pockets that banker up in Prairieton will need to pay the reward. But I'm talkin' about you." Loosely shifted in the chair again, this time allowing his coat to sag so that the ivory-butted six-gun showed. "Bein' hurt, if you jumped me, us alone in here, me bein' hurt an' you being in pretty good shape—"

Henry interrupted. "For the bank loot."

Loosely sucked on his cigar, let smoke drift upward, and slowly nodded his head.

Henry smiled bitterly at him. "You figure I came down in the last rain? I knock you senseless, take your gun, and rush out front for a horse, an' that son of a bitch of a sheriff shoots me in the back . . . and you get the money."

Loosely pondered. "Suppose you escaped out the back way?"

Henry felt like swearing. Loosely had all but admitted Mendenhall was indeed waiting out front. "I got a better idea," he told the tall, rawboned man. "You hand me your gun an' I'll poke it in your back when we walk out back."

Loosely did not meet Henry's gaze when he offered a belated reply. "I don't like losin' the gun. It's been with me—"

"Buy another one. There's enough bank loot to buy a whole run of 'em."

Two raised voices out front caught and held the attention of the men in the office. One voice, which Henry thought he'd heard before, said, "You can fetch him along, Sheriff. I got the Masonic Hall ready."

Mendenhall's reply was curt and gruff. "All right, Judge." Moments later Mendenhall opened the door but did not enter; he glared at both Henry and John Loosely. "The judge is ready." He scowled at the bounty hunter.

People on both sides of the road watched the procession. Those using the road turned off as far as they could to leave the middle of the road clear.

The three-man procession turned in at the lodge hall. Other townsmen drifted in.

Henry looked directly at the judge, whose head was bowed over an open book on the battered table.

People filed in, about equally divided between men and women. Several boys also tried to mingle with the people and were turned back by a large, stern man whose normal occupation was bossing the stage company's corralyard.

His Honor waited patiently until the large man closed the door and took a sentinel's stand in front of it, facing forward.

The judge looked out over the room. In a quiet, measured voice he explained the purpose of the hearing, said he would tolerate no loud talk among the spectators, then paused before striking a small block of wood with a gavel as he pronounced the court in session.

He paused again. The room was quiet, and all eyes were fixed on him as he said, "My name is Albert Flannery," and followed this announcement with instructions for Sheriff Mendenhall to hand over the charges. The room was silent as Judge Flannery leaned over to read.

When he was finished, he clasped both hands atop the paper the sheriff had given him and said, "Mister Mendenhall, do you have witnesses?"

The sheriff nodded in Loosely's direction "Yes, Your Honor. Mister John Loosely."

"Others, Sheriff?"

"No. If I had time I could maybe find some more."

Flannery gazed dispassionately at Sheriff Mendenhall. "Tell me something, Sheriff. You've listed a charge of horse stealing, is that right?"

"It's right."

"Where were those horses stolen, Sheriff?"

"Over at Barling Springs. Mister Loosely was over there an' found out—"

"Barling Springs has a sheriff?"

"No, sir. Where the horses was stolen they got a town marshal."

Flannery continued in his calm and measured tone of voice. "You've been to Barling Springs, have you?"

"Lots of times, Your Honor."

"So have I, Mister Mendenhall. As I remember, Barling Springs is in Washington County."

Sheriff Mendenhall's face was getting red. He had only just realized how this discussion was going.

"Sheriff, is Barling Springs in Washington County?"

"You just said it is."

Flannery continued to sit forward, hands clasped. He would have had to be blind not to recognize the signs of fury on Mendenhall's face. He let the silence run on for a while before speaking again.

"I'll summarize for you, Sheriff: You have a man on trial here for robbery, a serious crime. You have no witnesses; as far as I can see only Mister Loosely there is able to corroborate anything you've written in your report. But we're dealing with a robbery you allege but cannot substantiate with witnesses. And you are alleging horse theft which may or may not have happened. . . . Sheriff, the horse theft happened in Washington County. You have no more jurisdiction over there than I have. If the authorities in Washington County prefer charges and I'm assigned, I'll hold court in Washington County. . . . Sheriff, when you brought this prisoner to trial you committed yourself to abide by the decision of this court."

When the judge paused this time, Henry could feel the sheriff stiffen next to him. On Mendenhall's far side, John Loosely was mopping off sweat.

Flannery gazed over the still and silent room, then returned his attention to Sheriff Mendenhall. The judge did not raise his voice nor increase the measured manner of his words when he looked steadily at the sheriff and gave his judgment. "There simply is nothing here but allegations; hearsay; no proof, no witnesses to any crime having been committed in your bailiwick. . . . Case dismissed."

The judge struck the block of wood again with his gavel, when Henry felt Mendenhall coming out of his chair. Henry had already seen enough of Mendenhall's ungovernable temper to know what was coming.

Henry swung sideways as he was arising and bumped him off balance as the sheriff was raising his six-gun. Mendenhall stumbled over John Loosely's legs and was going to fall, but as he started down he turned the six-gun on Henry. Mendenhall was in the act of cocking it when Henry kicked out, missed the rising gun, but struck the arm behind it at the elbow.

Sheriff Mendenhall was scrabbling at the floor to arise when Henry grabbed Loosely's ivory-butted six-gun from the bounty hunter's holster.

He cocked the gun the exact moment Sheriff Mendenhall was raising his own hammer, while balancing his body off the floor with his left hand.

It sounded like two shots in one, but Henry beat the sheriff to it by a second.

Henry's bullet hit Sheriff Mendenhall in the gut, causing him to drop the gun and collapse. But the sheriff's own bullet had already struck flesh and bone. The shock of impact brought John Loosely straight up and out of his chair. His close-set eyes fixed on Judge Flannery before both knees turned loose and he fell.

CHAPTER TWENTY-ONE
The Big Bend

INSIDE THE MASONIC Hall, the large sentry was hurled aside by panicked people clawing to get out of the building.

Up front, the judge was too startled and too shocked to move.

Henry put Loosely's weapon on the judge's table, then turned to kneel beside Loosely. The bounty hunter had taken that wild shot in the right side through the heart.

The corralyard boss came forward, wearing a scowl. He stopped at the sight of the dead men. Judge Flannery, having regained some composure, looked at Henry without saying a word until the corralyard boss growled at him. "Your Honor, everybody knew Mendenhall couldn't control his temper. But I never thought he'd fly off the handle like this. Tryin' to kill a judge—and in front of everybody!"

The judge looked away from the corpses with a real effort, still unable to speak. The big, burly man quietly said, "Well, I'll find some fellers an' we'll haul 'em down to the icehouse. . . . Judge, this was the luckiest day of your life. If this feller hadn't seen it coming, Mendenhall would have killed you."

The corralyard boss walked solidly toward the roadway, his footfalls the only sound until they faded completely, leaving only the judge and Henry Malden.

Flannery said, "You're free to go, Mister Malden. My wife and I owed you. The sheriff just made it easier by wanting you tried for things he couldn't prove and which happened in a different county."

Henry nodded, eyed the judge for a moment, then said, "How is she?"

". . . Oh, my wife? She's doing fine. I probably shouldn't mention this, but she told me early this morning she and our little boy owe you their lives."

Henry was going to pass that off; he was not convinced the woman would not have been able to deliver the baby without help: it hadn't been much different from a cow calving. But before he could speak, Judge Flannery spoke again.

"She's very dear to me. She said I had to find a way to pay the debt." His Honor smiled feebly; there were still two dead men nearby. "I told her my job was to uphold the law. She told me if I didn't find a way to help you . . . well, I couldn't do it, Mister Malden, until I read the sheriff's report. So I guess I've repaid the debt."

Henry made a thin smile. "An' upheld the law. Before I leave town, would you mind if I saw her?"

His Honor looked past where four men were trooping in grimly from out front. He stood up again to lean on the table. "Not at all. She'd like that. Room four up at the hotel."

Henry turned to depart; the four men nodded to him, he nodded back, and did not turn to see what they were doing even after he was in the doorway where sunlight sparkled.

There were small clutches of people standing here and there the length of Leesville's main thoroughfare. Some saw him and stopped talking to stare. Across the road a man wearing a saddler's apron was standing in a doorway. He nodded as Henry crossed the road in his direction, but faded quickly back into his shop as Henry reached his side of the road and turned in the direction of the hotel.

Room four was only a short distance inside the old building. Henry knocked, was told to enter, and was surprised to find the woman he had once thought was heavyset sitting in a chair holding her baby, who was asleep.

She asked in a worried voice what the gunfire had been about. He told her without mentioning the very strong possibility that Mendenhall had intended to shoot her husband.

When she asked about her husband Henry pulled off his hat and said, "He's fine."

They looked steadily at one another through an awkward moment before she spoke again. "Here," she said, handing him a key. "It goes to the lock on the carriage shed out back. Your saddlebags are under the bedding in the wagon."

The baby made soft whimpering sounds and burrowed closer against his mother.

The woman soothed the child and studied Henry for a moment before speaking again. "I'm very curious, Mister Malden." When Henry remained silent and expressionless she asked, "Did you do what they said you did?"

"I'm sorry to say I did, ma'am."

"Well . . . whatever else you've done, you helped us more than I can say. I'll never forget you."

Henry leaned to gently touch the baby's head, nodded, and left the room.

The carriage house out back stood well apart from any other structure. He unlocked the door and entered a shadowy large shed with a musty smell. The repaired wagon took up most of the room.

Henry approached it, stopped to listen, then rummaged until he found the saddlebags. If they had been opened there was no sign of it. He did not believe the woman had looked inside them.

The sun was almost directly overhead. Henry rode east the way he had been traveling with Buff before the storm. It did not much matter now whether he left tracks or not, nor did he worry about it, or the fact that he had no shell belt, belt gun, or Winchester in the empty scabbard under his saddle fender.

When nightfall overtook him, Henry was halfway up a curving sidehill where twisted pines grew. He hobbled the horse in a small meadow and built a warming fire. He was not hungry. Later, he did not sleep well either, between having to feed twigs into the little fire and being bedeviled by his memories.

In the morning he headed east again. He had a destination. It was not the one he'd had a few weeks back. It was probably better: the Big Bend country of south Texas was rugged, wild, sparsely inhabited, and had plenty of feed and water. If the law from Prairieton came nosing around, a man could hole up in secret places left by Indians, or he could ride down over the line into Mexico. The stories were that hunted men could hide out down there for years—even for a lifetime.